The Weekend

MIKE WHITEHEAD

ARCHWAY
PUBLISHING

Archway Publishing books may be ordered through booksellers or by contacting:

Archway Publishing
1663 Liberty Drive
Bloomington, IN 47403
www.archwaypublishing.com
844-669-3957

ISBN: 978-1-4808-9980-3 (sc)
ISBN: 978-1-4808-9981-0 (e)

Library of Congress Control Number: 2020923112

Print information available on the last page.

Archway Publishing rev. date: 12/23/2020

For Martha

Part I

Friday Evening

Chapter 1

S'am Roberts rang the doorbell and went into full panic mode. This was a crazy, stupid idea. What was he thinking? If Maggie didn't answer, he would run, not walk, back to his car and get out of there as fast as possible.

Too late. The door swung open, and Maggie McWilliams Duncan was staring straight at him.

"You probably don't remember me, but ..."

Before Sam could finish the sentence, everything went black. His six-foot-two-inch frame began to crumble. He often thought of falling into Maggie's arms, but fainting wasn't what Sam had in mind. Maggie couldn't hold him, and both of them landed on the cherry hardwood entryway floor.

It took a minute or two for Sam to open his eyes. It only took forty-something years for this meeting to happen, and it couldn't have gotten off to a worse start.

"Are you all right?" Maggie asked as she knelt over him.

Sam rubbed his forehead and tried to focus. He was more embarrassed than hurt. So many times, Sam lay awake at night thinking of this moment. What he would say, and how would he say it? Now that the fantasy was transformed into reality, Sam's lips couldn't form a single word, much less come up with a great opening line.

"That certainly was an entrance I'll never forget," Maggie continued. "This is a surprise in so many ways. How have you been, Sam? It's been a very long time."

She did remember him! Sam just stared at Maggie. Like a lump of dumb, he just stared at her. Everything he felt was in his head, but he couldn't push the right button to get a sentence to rush out.

"I think we should get you to a doctor!" Maggie said.

"No, no I'll be fine," he shot back, trying to get up off the floor. "Just give me a second."

When he got to his feet, Sam was happy nothing was broken, except maybe his pride. "I'm sorry."

"Don't give it a second thought," Maggie said. "Let me get a good look at you, Sam Roberts. Are you at least going to say hello? This reminds me of the first time you called all those years ago. You didn't have much to say then either."

Sam couldn't help but notice that Maggie still looked great. Sure, her hair was much shorter, and there were a few wrinkles around her eyes, but nothing more than what you would normally earn from fifty-eight years and two children. She still had that tiny figure, sparkling eyes, and warm smile. She looked stylish in her solid white top and lavender jeans.

"Forgive me for showing up unannounced," Sam said. "I was in the neighborhood, and I thought I would say hello. Am I interrupting anything?"

"Not many people are in this neighborhood, Sam, but I'm glad you are here. Can you stay for a little while? It has been a long time, hasn't it?"

"That might have been a little white lie," Sam said. "I wanted to come say hello and see how you are doing. You really remember our first phone call?"

"Where has the time gone?" Maggie seemed to be saying more to herself than Sam. "It seems like only yesterday we were children. Now I have grown children. We have a lot of catching up to do—unless you have to rush off to an important sporting event?"

"You know about my work? Well, my previous work." Sam didn't know if Maggie knew the latest news about his life. "I'm impressed."

"Let me shut the door before the neighbors wonder about this strange man who threw himself at me."

"I'm so—"

"No more apologies," Maggie said.

The old Victorian house was even more elegant on the inside than it was on the outside. It was obvious Maggie had taken a lot of pride in making sure her stamp was in every room. Nothing gaudy or too fancy. More simple and elegant, much like Maggie herself.

The living room, with its original wooden shutters framing the huge window looking out onto the front yard, was filled with antiques. Her sofa, probably from the early 1900s, was off-white, with carved wooden legs. The two matching, classic brown, leather captain's chairs were a perfect complement to the walnut end table and crystal and porcelain lamp.

Sam decided to sit in one of the chairs facing the couch. "I apologize for stopping in like this. It's Friday night, and you could well have plans for this evening."

"It so happens that I don't have any plans tonight," she said. "You always did like to worry about things you couldn't control."

"Like you?"

"Like me. I want you to stay for dinner. You can stay for dinner, can't you?"

"That would be great, but ..."

"No conditions," Maggie said. "It's settled. I was going to stay home tonight anyway and read a book. So this is delightful. It gives me an excuse to cook. It won't be anything fancy. Just some pasta and a salad."

"That would be perfect—like someone I know." Sam told himself to be cautious about throwing around too many compliments too soon, but he couldn't help himself.

"You always were good with words—even as a young man," Maggie said.

"I do love words," Sam confessed. "Words allowed me to have a wonderful career. Before we go any further, I want to say how sorry I am about David. I'm sorry for you and your family."

"Thank you. I don't know why you wouldn't have heard about it. Everyone else in the world certainly has. It's been more than two years. I'm at peace with my husband's death."

Something in Maggie's voice didn't ring true for Sam. Had Maggie really come to grips with David's death or was she still trying to convince herself?

"I've only wanted good things to happen in your life," Sam said. "This was such a tragedy. I'm truly sorry."

"I know you are, Sam. I very much appreciate it. My girls are doing fine—that is the main thing. Would you like to see a photo of them?"

Before Sam could answer, Maggie was up and out of the room. Within thirty seconds, she returned with an eight-by-ten framed portrait of the twins.

"Lily is older than Lucy by seven minutes. It's hard to believe they are twenty-five years old."

"I guess that means we are getting old," Sam said, making sure Maggie saw the playful grin on his face.

"Speak for yourself! I suppose I shouldn't have spoiled them so much, but I couldn't help it." As she spoke, Maggie's eyes never left the photo.

For Sam it brought back a flood of memories. These young women looked just like their mother at that age. Only there were two of them.

It had been more than forty years since Sam met Maggie. To be exact, it had been forty years, one month, and twelve days. They were both eighteen, although Sam was seven days older than Maggie.

Within the first three minutes of their initial telephone conversation, he was in love. Actually, that first conversation lasted all of three minutes.

He had been invited to a formal dance at her Catholic high school. He didn't know many kids at that school, but he wanted to wear his new white tux jacket. Sam had never been to a country club; he was curious about the people who were rich enough to go there for golf, tennis, dinner, and social events.

Sam had gotten Maggie's name and telephone number from a friend of a friend. It took him several days to work up the courage to call. He never would have called if he had known he was about to talk with the most popular girl in the school. Sometimes ignorance is bliss. He had the entire conversation planned in his mind. At least, it was planned until Maggie said hello.

"You don't know me," he began, "but I got your name from Emily at your school, and I was just wondering if you would be interested ..."

"Maybe you can start by telling me your name," Maggie said. "I guess you know mine."

"I'm sorry." Sam was thankful Maggie couldn't see all the various shades of red on his face. "I'm Sam Roberts. I go to Forest Park."

"Nice to meet you, Sam Roberts."

"I'm planning on coming to the dance at your school in a couple of months, so I thought I would call and introduce myself."

"Be sure to come find me and say hello in person."

"I promise."

"See you at the dance."

"Good night."

Thirty-seven words. That's all Maggie said, but it was more than enough. That voice would forever be imprinted on his mind. Sam knew, instinctively knew, someone like Maggie was too special to be taken for granted.

The twins had Maggie's same confident smile, the same twinkle in their dark brown eyes, and the same silky chestnut hair.

"They look just like me when I was their age, don't they?" Maggie snapped Sam out of his trance.

"Lucy and Lily are almost as beautiful, but not quite."

"You always were too kind, Sam."

"When it comes to you, Maggie, it's true. Maybe I should have pretended I didn't care."

Maggie decided it was best to simply ignore his remark. "So would you like to sit and relax for a bit while I prepare dinner—or do you want to be brave and come into the kitchen with me?"

"I'm feeling brave tonight," Sam said. "Show me the way."

Maggie's kitchen, down the hall from the living room, looked like something out of a magazine. While her Victorian home definitely was more Shakespeare than Shakira, the kitchen was a nice blend of the old and new. The same hardwood floors Sam saw in the living room continued into the kitchen, but all the countertops, including the island countertop, had been updated with a cream granite mixed with flecks of gold. The light solid-wood cabinets blended well with the modern Viking gas range, refrigerator, and double oven. Even the microwave was Viking.

Sam wasn't the greatest cook, but he knew top-of-the-line appliances. An array of pots, pans, and iron skillets hung from the ceiling, like moss hanging from the trees in south Louisiana. A lot of time and attention went into designing and updating Maggie's kitchen. It was impressive, to say the least.

"So catch me up on your life, Sam," Maggie said as she retrieved the lettuce, tomato, and cucumber from the refrigerator. "Married? Kids? Is your job still exciting?"

"No, no, and no."

"You went way too fast for me. And there's much more to life than one-word answers, you know."

"I'm not married, and I don't have any children. My job was exciting; actually, I have been doing something completely different these days."

"You aren't married—or you have never been married?" Maggie knew there was a big difference.

"I've never been married," Sam admitted.

"I don't believe it, Sam. You are handsome and smart, not to mention charismatic. And you've never been married?" Sam did look amazing in his blue polo and khaki pants.

"I've come close a couple of times, but I've never met

the right woman." For Sam, the right woman was standing right in front of him slicing a tomato, but there was no way he was about to admit that to Maggie. "I would have loved to have had children, but you've got to have a wife first."

"Not in the twenty-first century," Maggie noted, a slight grin crossing her face.

"Great point. I would prefer to have a wife and then kids. I'm too old now."

"Too old to have children—or too old to get married?" Maggie was not going to let this go.

"I would get married … if all the stars aligned. At my age, children aren't an option. I've missed my window of opportunity."

"That's too bad; you would have been a great dad."

"I would like to think so, but you never know until you are going toe-to-toe with teenagers."

"You are preaching to the choir, but I wouldn't take anything in the world for Lily and Lucy. Tell me about your career. I've never been a big sports fan, but are you still doing all that television sports stuff?"

"No, I gave it up about three years ago. I've been a missionary in the Amazon for the past several years."

"Oh my God, didn't some network do a special on you? I vaguely remember something about a broadcaster giving up his career to do that kind of work. I didn't pay much attention at the time. I guess they were talking about you." Maggie felt embarrassed for two reasons. First, she had to admit she didn't keep up with sporting events, and second, she hadn't realized it was Sam.

"Actually, *60 Minutes* did something. Everyone thought I was crazy for walking away."

"You weren't crazy, were you, Sam?" Maggie finished the salad, put it back in the refrigerator, and began to cook the pasta. She had already made some homemade sauce.

"I don't think so. I don't regret my decision in the least."

"I'm more than intrigued; I'm fascinated. I'm not going to feed you until you promise to tell me all about your life. You are too modest for your own good."

"That's always been my problem with you, Maggie. I've always been too reserved around you. I think it's because I've always put you on a pedestal."

"Pedestals are very dangerous places to be," Maggie said. "At some point, everyone falls off and shatters. By the time this evening is over, I predict I won't be on a pedestal any longer."

"How about we make a deal, Maggie? I told myself that I was going to tell you the truth. So, if I promise to tell you the truth, do you promise to tell me the truth?"

"I'll do my best, but, David …" her voice trailed off. "Down deep, I'm still a little raw."

"I thought you were trying to be brave earlier when you said you were doing fine," he said. "I understand. No matter what happens while I'm here tonight, I want to be open and honest with you. I'm hoping you can do the same."

"We aren't eighteen years old any longer, Sam. A lot has happened to both of us, but I haven't done anything I'm not willing to share. You just need to give me a little time."

"I'm not here to interrogate you, Maggie. I promise. I want this to go well. I know you are vulnerable."

"The nice thing about being our age," Maggie said, "is that we don't have to care what other people think about us. We can be ourselves. Do what we want—within reason. Say what we want. Being comfortable in your own skin is part of the journey of life."

"Your skin looks pretty good from here," Sam said. "And tanned." He always loved the fact that Maggie had that beautiful olive complexion so many people wanted.

"Before we get into this too deeply, let's eat," Maggie said, draining the pasta and placing it in a simple blue and white serving bowl. The sauce was bubbling on the stove; she put a generous helping in a smaller bowl that was part of the same set. "Do you want to go to the dining room or stay in the kitchen?"

"I would rather stay right here … if it's okay with you. I like your breakfast table. It's just the right size for two people." In fact, there wasn't much about Maggie's house that Sam didn't like.

Like the perfect hostess, Maggie placed the bowls on the small, antique oak table. She quickly went to the refrigerator to collect the salad she had made. Sam helped set the table, smiling a little as Maggie handed him the good china. They worked in concert and in silence. It was comfortable, even pleasant. More like a compliment than anything else. Like two people who knew each other so well that they didn't have to talk with each other every minute they were together.

"Do you mind if I light a candle?" she asked.

"I think that would be quite nice, actually," Sam said.

"I was hoping you wouldn't mind; it's been so long since I've used them."

"I'm quite used to candles," Sam admitted. "I've eaten by candlelight many times in the past few years. We used them for light since we often didn't have any electricity. Not exactly romantic."

"So what's been going on the last forty years or so, Sam?"

"That might take a couple of years. The salad and pasta are excellent. Thanks so much."

"Thank you. How about this? Start from your most recent adventure."

"My work in South America?"

"Yes, I can't imagine living anywhere unless I know I can get my nails done."

Sam couldn't help but laugh out loud. "It's hard to explain, but I fell in love with the people of Brazil when I went there a few years ago on an assignment. That trip changed my life. I came back and made arrangements to move there permanently."

"Brazil is a big country." Maggie didn't know how big, but she remembered her high school geography teacher saying it was one of the biggest countries in the world.

"At first, I thought about moving to Rio de Janeiro. It's a beautiful city, and it's near the ocean. I was going to write books by day and stroll the beach by sunset."

"The girls and I have fallen in love with the beach, too. Every year, we would go to Gulf Shores in Alabama. Do you know that area? Pure white beaches—and you can drive there in a day."

"Yes. I would love to live in Destin, but Gulf Shores would be a good option."

"I thought you were going to live in Rio?"

Sam couldn't help but notice how beautiful Maggie looked on the opposite side of the table bathed in soft candlelight.

"Actually, I never made it to Rio. I found a Catholic mission program that does social justice work in the western part of Brazil … in the Amazon region. I've always been fascinated with the Amazon, even as a boy. The people, the work, the Amazon. It was a great fit."

"I'm dying to ask a million personal questions." Maggie didn't like gossiping or prying into anyone's person life, especially since David had died, but she decided to take a chance.

"Sure. Ask away."

"Why did you give up such a great career? And why missionary work?"

"I wish I had a dollar for every time I've been asked those two questions," Sam said.

"I'm sorry. I understand if you don't want to talk about it."

"No, no. I don't mind at all. I did have a great career. The network sent me all over the world to cover sporting events. It was a dream job. I covered Super Bowls, the World Series, and the Olympics, but something was missing. Sports was fun, but I wanted to do more. If I hadn't gone to Brazil to cover soccer, I never would have discovered a new way of thinking about the world. Most of all, I wouldn't have discovered a nation of people I have grown to love."

"I'm sure there are a lot of people who would kill to have that kind of job. The money had to be a nice bonus."

"The money was great, no doubt. I knew I had a great

career. I loved the work, and I always gave 100 percent. It was just time to move on to something else."

"That something else was missionary work? There were a lot of other things you could have done."

"When I was making preparations to go back to Brazil, you know, to write books, I had an epiphany. Some people refer to it as a calling. If I really wanted to do something meaningful, I could work for the church. Writing novels would have been fun—and fulfilling—but I can do that any time. I found a missionary group that's stationed in Brazil and applied. The rest is history."

"I bet you can't wait to get back," Maggie said. "You must miss them very much."

"I've fulfilled my obligation to the program, but I would go back. There might be a reason I would stay in the States." Sam stared straight into Maggie's eyes.

Maggie let his comment float in the air. "Tell me about the people."

It was obvious to Sam that Maggie wasn't ready to be the focus of his attention. No rush. It had taken him a few decades to get to this point. What was a little more time? "The Brazilians are so generous," he said between bites of pasta. "They have very little in the way of material goods. No medicine. Very little good drinking water. No electricity. They have enough food to get them through the day—but little else. No matter how little they have, they will give you anything and everything they have."

Sam was looking for a sign that he was boring Maggie, but she still seemed interested. She pushed her plate back, rested her elbows on the table, and waited for him to continue.

"When you visit a family, they always will share their food with you," Sam said, "even if it means everyone in the house has to have a smaller portion. It's humbling, to say the least. Anyway, enough about me. Tell me how you are doing."

"You know the old cliche, Sam. Time heals everything—or at least time is supposed to heal everything. It's been two years since David's death, and I'm definitely doing better today than I was two years ago. At first, I will admit, it was a struggle, especially with the girls. I still have some healing to do."

"When we are young," Sam said, "we think everyone will live forever, including our parents."

"I should have seen it coming, Sam. In my gut, I knew something was wrong with David. I just didn't know how wrong. Sometimes I blame myself for not being able to get him some help. Isn't that the biggest irony of all? I should have gotten a therapist for the therapist."

"You don't have to talk about this," Sam said.

"It's okay," Maggie said. "I want to tell you. Intellectually, you know it's not your fault, but you still beat yourself up. I did get some help—and now I am much, much better."

"You always were a strong person."

"Some days are better than others, but I'm having many more good days than bad days. I try to stay strong for the girls."

"Tell me about Lucy and Lily."

"After graduation—with honors, I might add—they decided to join the Peace Corps. I guess they just wanted to get away, and I can't blame them. They are having a great time."

"Don't tell me they are in Brazil?" That would be too much of a coincidence.

"No," Maggie said, laughing out loud. "They are in Asia. Thailand. I worry about them, but they assure me they are safe."

"And you? What about you, Maggie?"

"I still teach a course or two at the university. I guess you could say I'm semiretired. I took a year off after David died. Now, I just don't want to go back full-time anymore."

"Maybe I can phrase it another way, Maggie. How are you deep down in your heart?"

"That is deep, indeed, Mr. Roberts. That will require a

much longer answer." Maggie reached for Sam's empty plate. "Let me clean up the kitchen, and I promise to answer you."

No way Sam was going to let Maggie clean up the kitchen by herself. It was actually quite easy—a couple of plates, a couple of glasses, one dishwasher, and they were done. Sam had an ulterior motive for wanting to help. He wanted to hear Maggie's story, and the clock was ticking. He didn't know how the evening was going to end, but he wanted one thing for sure—he wanted Maggie to know how he felt.

Maggie brewed a pot of decaffeinated tea and took it to the living room. She settled in on the couch, scrunching her legs under her body.

Sam decided to nestle into one of the deep, brown leather captain's chairs next to Maggie. "Don't feel obligated to say a word," Sam said, hoping she wouldn't take his offer. "I shouldn't be so nosy. None of this is my business."

"Nonsense," Maggie said. "You are an old friend. We should be able to confide in each other. Besides, since I don't know anyone in the Amazon, please feel free to tell anyone you like."

"I can't argue with that logic." Sam laughed so hard his tea sloshed over his cup and settled in his saucer.

"When I wake up every morning, I thank God for giving

me another day," Maggie said. "And when I go to bed, I ask God to remind me why bad things happen to good people."

"Bad things happen to good people because bad things happen to good people," Sam said. "There really is no explanation. It isn't God's will; he doesn't want bad things to happen. We live in a world where bad people sometimes have great lives—and great people have crummy lives. It's not very complicated. All of us suffer at some point. It's how we face and fight through that suffering that counts."

"I don't know God's plan for me," Maggie said. "It seems like there is something more I should be doing, but I don't know what it is."

"So something is missing?"

"You can tell you are a former reporter—always asking the right follow-up question at the right time. Yes, something is missing. Maybe. I don't know. It's just a feeling I have sometimes. Nothing specific. Nothing I can pinpoint."

"I can relate to what you are saying. I went through something similar—until I figured out where God was leading me." For Sam, there still was a missing piece to his life's puzzle, and she was sitting across from him. What he had at that very moment was what he wanted every day for the rest of his life. For some people, marriage was monotonous and repetitious. For him, it would be like eating chocolate ice cream. He would never grow tired of being with Maggie.

"I know I shouldn't complain because I do have a good life. I'm not wealthy by any means. In fact, far from it. This house is the only thing David left me. I didn't know it at the time, but we were pretty much broke when he died. Thank goodness I had enough in savings to bury him, but I have two great kids, I'm healthy now, and I have good friends. And I have a job."

"What do you mean healthy now?" Sam thought that was an interesting turn of phrase.

"Well, I can see you really are listening. About twenty years ago, I had a minor skirmish with cancer. It took a couple of years and a team of doctors, but I have been in remission ever since."

"I'm so sorry to hear that news, but I'm glad it's old news and that you are much better now," Sam said. "That's scary. I know what you mean about health. It's everything. I've been in pretty good shape myself, not counting my one battle with malaria. Thank God, it wasn't a severe case."

"It sounds horrible."

"When I had it, I didn't know if I was going to live or die," Sam said. "I'm such a baby."

"Most men are." Maggie couldn't help herself.

"In the end, I didn't have any permanent damage from it. Enough about me. This is your story, not mine."

"I'm trying to figure out who I am. Somewhere along the way, I lost the old me. It's sort of like not feeling the warmth of the sun for a week. Or somehow going from winter to summer without experiencing the joy of spring. Or going to church and not singing. It's hard to pinpoint, but you can feel it when there is something missing in your soul."

"I think it's getting too deep for our own good," Sam said. "Maybe we should change the subject."

"I'm sorry," Maggie said. "I didn't serve dessert."

"Wow, Maggie, that is changing the subject. Why don't we do something about dessert. How about going for some ice cream?"

"I really shouldn't. My girlish figure, you know."

"I shouldn't either, but you have to have a little fun in life. Do you still like chocolate?"

"Yes, but I haven't had it in ages."

"Then my treat. Is there an ice cream shop in Natchitoches?"

"Yes, but I think it closes at ten."

"We have thirty minutes."

"It does sound like fun," Maggie said. "Just give me a minute."

Even at nine thirty on an August night, the temperature was still close to ninety-five degrees. That was one unique characteristic about the South—it was hot during the day and just as hot when the sun went down. Couple the heat with humidity, and you have nature's version of a sauna. The weather was perfect for Sam. He liked it hot. The hotter, the better. Good thing too because it was going to be hot for days to come. That was one thing Brazil and Louisiana had in common—the temperature went from hot to hotter.

Baskin-Robbins didn't close until ten on Friday and Saturday, so Sam and Maggie made it in plenty of time. The drive from her house took all of ten minutes. Both of them settled on a scoop of chocolate in a cup. They were purists. No gummy bears, no white chocolate chips, no sprinkles or flakes, or any other tantalizing treat that might take away from the pure chocolate taste. The teenager behind the counter was probably wondering if he should offer these two cute old people a senior discount.

Maggie and Sam decided to sit on the outside patio at a small wrought iron table, enjoying each scrumptious bite. That moment reminded Sam of the short time they dated so many years ago. Those teen years when he fell in love for the first—and only—time in his life.

As he watched Maggie twirl her spoon around her cup

and gently savor each bite of her ice cream, Sam replayed that magical summer before they left for college.

He remembered Maggie's confident laugh, teeth white as snow, and the way she held his hand as they walked down the street. Somehow, her hand was a perfect fit for his. He remembered the way he would hug her when she cried for no reason. Mostly, he recalled the way he hugged her when she needed comfort.

The best times that summer were spent in a park near Maggie's home. They would sit on a park bench—or she would bring her grandmother's homemade quilt for them to sit on under one of the giant maple trees. It was there that Sam told Maggie of his dreams. He was planning on saving the world someday. If he couldn't save the world, surely he could change it for the better. He didn't know exactly how or when, or even why, but that was his dream. The only thing better to Sam than saving the planet was sharing his dream with Maggie.

Maggie had dreams, too. She wanted to be a dancer. Maybe she would be a ballet dancer in Europe or part of a Broadway dance company in New York City. Audiences would come from around the globe to see her perform, amazed at her athleticism, grace, and elegance.

Dreams are so plentiful when you are young. That is the joy of youth, but there are different kinds of dreams. Some dreams last a lifetime. Some last a day or two. Some dreams are wonderful; some dreams are called nightmares. For Sam, his dream of being with Maggie lasted his entire life.

As they were sharing ice cream, Sam was all about the future, but just for a moment, he had to go back to the past. It was a rekindling of a summertime memory of long ago.

"Maggie, do you remember how many nights we had ice cream during our summer together? A lot," Sam said before Maggie had a chance to answer.

"That's when our metabolism allowed us to eat anything we wanted."

Sam knew Maggie was right. "We may have shared a chocolate shake, but we shared so much more."

"What happened to your dream of becoming a professional dancer?" Sam could still recall the one time he saw Maggie performing in her summer dance recital. He was biased, but she was so talented. If he were casting a principal dancer, Maggie would be at the top of the list.

"Thanks for bringing that up," Maggie said half joking and half serious. "I majored in dance in college, and I thought I might have had a chance to land with a great company, but I crash-landed one time too many and snapped my ankle.

I really was never the same again. That's how you go from Broadway dreams to teaching."

"Life does get in the way of our dreams, but there's nothing wrong with teaching. You touch a lot of young lives."

"That's what I kept telling myself all these years. I don't know if it's true or just a rationalization on my part. And if my memory serves me correctly, Sam, you were going to change the world—or at least a small part of it."

"Like I said, life gets in the way. It's very difficult to save anyone when you spend most of your life covering sports. You can make a lot of people happy, but you seldom transform societies."

"I guess both of us are failures."

Sam couldn't help but smile. "You could call me a failure, but not you, Maggie. I don't know your two children, but from what you've told me, I bet they are wonderful young people. If you have two great kids, you are anything but a failure."

"That's nice of you to say, Sam."

"It's true; don't forget it. We better get back; it's definitely past my bedtime," Sam said, taking the final bite of chocolate.

By the time they arrived at Maggie's house, it was almost ten thirty. For Sam, it was a great evening. He didn't know how the night would end, but Sam wanted Maggie to remember their time together as a good thing and not a bad thing. He didn't know what to do or what to say. He didn't want to say something wrong or do something wrong.

"I have a favor to ask," Sam said as Maggie unlocked her front door. "Can you give me directions to a hotel?"

Maggie turned to face him. "If I ask you to come in, do you promise not to pass out again?"

"I'll try my best, but it's getting late. I did have a great time."

"I had fun, too, but I've got to ask you—why did you come here this evening? Did you just want to say hello and be on your way? I don't understand you at all."

"I don't know what to say, Maggie."

"How about the truth, Sam?"

"The way I felt about you forty years ago is the same way I feel today. I just didn't want to come here and have you think I'm some kind of maniac who's one card short of a full deck."

"This is a little strange for both of us, but I'm betting you are a good guy. In fact, I insist you stay here tonight. No need to go to a hotel, although we have some terrific bed-and-breakfast inns in Natchitoches. I have four bedrooms, and three of them aren't being used. I'll be insulted if you don't stay here. Besides, you are right. It's late, and I'll feel better if you aren't driving around at night, trying to find a place to stay. Go get your gear."

"Yes, ma'am. You don't have to ask me twice. I'll get my things out of my rental." When he came back in, he heard Maggie calling his name from the back of the house.

"The guest bedroom is back here, Sam." Maggie was fluffing the pillows on the bed when he found his room. "Get some sleep, and we can talk in the morning."

"Good night, and thanks for everything."

Sam was hoping Maggie would ask him to stay. His prayer had been answered, but it was even more important to him to do the right thing and not put any pressure on her. He didn't know where the next day would take him, but he was willing to find out.

Even though it had been a great evening, Sam was glad to crawl under the covers. He quickly discovered he was exhausted, but he couldn't seem to go to sleep. He lay in the dark thinking about Maggie.

"Tell me why you really came here today," Maggie said, flipping on the light in Sam's room.

Sam shot straight up in bed, wondering if he were somehow dreaming.

Maggie, in a light blue terry cloth bathrobe, stood at the foot of his bed. "Why are you here, Sam?"

Here was the moment of truth. Come hell or high water,

Sam was determined to get it right this time. Nothing phony, nothing exaggerated, just the simple, honest truth. Look-her-in the-eyes truth. Take-a-risk-and-go-for-it truth. Sam knew his words had to come from the heart.

Maggie sat on the edge of the bed, waiting for Sam's response.

He sat back against the headboard and tried to collect his thoughts. He took full measure of Maggie's face and marveled how lovely she was, even without her makeup. Certainly, he would admit to being anything but objective, but Maggie was even more beautiful than when he first met her so long ago.

"I've dreamed of this day for forty years," Sam began. "I've played it and replayed it over and over in my mind. What I would say? What would you say? I didn't have it all figured out, but my dream definitely had a happy ending. As strange as it may sound, I never gave up on the idea of us being together. Everyone thinks I am crazy. I'm not exaggerating. Everyone thinks I'm crazy. So, after a while, I didn't talk about my personal life. I just became Sam Roberts, confirmed bachelor."

"You never came close to getting married?" Maggie asked.

"Sure. As you said, time really does heal everything. I dated off and on over the years. It's easy not to get close to anyone, especially when you travel all the time like I did.

I threw myself into my work. Women thought what I did was pretty cool, but they never got to know me. Mostly, I didn't want to know them either. There was one time I was engaged, but I just couldn't pull the trigger because I didn't love her enough to spend the rest of my life with her."

What Sam couldn't say, at least not yet, was that over all these years, he kept coming back to the same place. Maggie was the one for him, and he wasn't going to settle for someone he didn't completely love. Ever since they were in high school, he hoped they could be together someday. It crushed him when Maggie told him she wanted to date other people in college, but he thought he would get another shot at some point.

"David was the first guy I dated when I went to college, and I ended up marrying him. Who knew?"

Sam was ashamed to say it out loud, but he had some horrible thoughts throughout his life. Sometimes he even said a small prayer that Maggie might get divorced. In Sam's deepest, darkest moments, he hoped her husband would have a heart attack or a car wreck. There were one or two nights he had to beg God to forgive him. He never really wanted anything bad to happen to David—and certainly not to Maggie.

"There were times since David's death that I wished we had been divorced. Didn't you ever think what you thought was love was just a teenage crush?"

"Yes, I thought I might be having a mental meltdown. I did go to a therapist to sort out my feelings. At one point, my therapist even suggested I find you and settle this once and for all. She was sure I would see you weren't as pretty as I remembered, as smart as I remembered, or as nice as I remembered."

"Did you ever think about coming, Sam?"

"I did come. I sat right in front of your house, trying to get the nerve to come to the door. It was years ago. After two hours of being frozen in my front seat, I drove back to the airport and left. I couldn't see you. That's probably why I fainted this time. Believe it or not, I couldn't do it to David and your kids. Not that I thought you would pack a bag and leave with me. I didn't want to be the one to cause trouble in your marriage. Even if I could break up your marriage, I would always be the bad guy with your children. And you. Every time you looked at me, you would know that it was my fault your kids were miserable by taking them away from their dad. Actually, I didn't know what to think."

"Life can certainly take some strange twists and turns, can't it? I thought David and I would live out our lives relatively content. Sometimes I think I should have done something different. Sometimes I think I should have seen the signs. Something."

"Over the years, I had to come to terms with you and your

family," Sam said. "I threw myself into my career, and then, in the past few years, I found something that was almost as exciting as you—Brazil. It wasn't the country; it was the people. They are so warm and kind and loving. They gave me a purpose for living. I believe my work made a difference—for the people and for me. They helped me grow—just as much as I helped them. My work in the Amazon replaced the love I wanted from you but couldn't have. Honestly, I have been content for the past several years."

"I'm glad you were there, Sam. That is much more important than being here with me."

"I can go back whenever I want. My contract was up a year ago, but I decided to stay in the mission field. I have a deal with my priest there. I can stay as long as I like, or I can leave when I like. Father Paul has been good to me. My world changed when a friend sent me the newspaper clipping about David. It took a very long time to reach me, but it didn't take me nearly as long to decide to come here."

"And now that you are here?"

"Once I got here, my heart started to race. Those old feelings resurfaced, and it was like I was eighteen again. When I arrived, it was like I had been frozen all those years, and when the ice melted, nothing had changed, especially you. Before you say anything, let me assure you, my feelings and thought process are much more mature than that of a teenager."

"I must tell you my ego could use a boost. Needless to say, my self-esteem has taken a beating the past couple of years." Maggie stopped short of telling him what she was really thinking because she was trying to sort it out herself. She did know one thing—from the moment Sam fainted in her entry, she was attracted to him. And the more he talked, the more she was impressed.

"I promise, 95 percent of the women in the world wish they looked as good as you."

A tear ran down Maggie's face. She took a deep breath. "You took a risk by coming here today, Sam, so I'm going to take a risk now." Maggie took off her robe and let it drop to the floor, revealing a blue cotton nightgown with tiny yellow flowers. She pulled back the covers on the side of the bed opposite Sam and slid in next to him.

"This has been a crazy day," Sam said, shaking his head. "Are you sure you can handle this?"

"I don't know, but I do know I like being next to you. Can I ask you something, Sam?"

"Sure, anything."

"And you will be honest with me?"

"I'll do my best."

"Can I use one of your pillows?"

Sam smiled, shook his head, and tossed Maggie a pillow. "Can we try something? Will you trust me?"

"My mother told me never to trust a man, and as it turns out, she was absolutely right."

Sam reached up and turned off the light and pulled Maggie and her pillow next to him, her head resting on his shoulder. "Go to sleep, young lady. Remember, we are old and tired."

"Tired, yes. Old, never."

"That's my Maggie."

Sam lay in the dark with Maggie next to him. He closed his eyes, drinking in her smell. Within a few minutes, he could tell she was asleep, and he could feel her breath on his chest. All his life, he had dreamed of this moment: in bed, holding Maggie in his arms until she fell asleep.

"I love you, Maggie," he said, knowing she didn't hear him. Sam had said it so many times over the years, so many times just before he went to sleep, and now his dream had come true. She was in his arms. "I love you."

Part II

Saturday Morning

Chapter 2

S'unlight splashed through the bedroom window and hit Sam in the face. It was a gentle, yet not-so-subtle wake-up call. He hadn't slept so soundly in years. He quickly glanced to his left. The covers were turned back, and Maggie was nowhere in sight. Since the sun was climbing in the morning sky, Sam reasoned it must be fairly late. He reached for his watch. It was a few minutes before ten.

The events of the night before were swirling in Sam's head. If he were making a movie, his night with Maggie was the perfect script. Casual dinner, great conversation, relaxed atmosphere. It was almost too perfect to be true. The fact that Maggie ended the night beside him in bed was a big bonus. Needless to say, it was a real shock, but he wasn't going to overanalyze the situation.

Sitting up in bed, it was the first time Sam had an opportunity to take a look at the guest bedroom. Like the rest of the Victorian home, the room was neatly appointed. The bed, nightstand, and armoire were vintage antiques. The dark walnut furniture contrasted nicely with the light yellow flower-patterned comforter and matching pillows. The walls were filled with original art, mostly beach scenes.

Sam decided to shower, shave, and brush his teeth before meeting the day—and Maggie. He wanted to look his best. Perhaps he could take her out for brunch or lunch, depending on her mood. He didn't know the possibilities in Natchitoches, Louisiana.

As soon as he was ready, he raced for the kitchen. No Maggie. He checked the living room where they had enjoyed each other's company just a few hours earlier. No Maggie. He hesitated for a moment, but then he decided to check her bedroom. No Maggie. He even called her name. No answer.

Then he saw her sitting in the backyard, rocking in a two-person swing with a forest green canopy. She was gently rocking back and forth, staring in the distance, looking at nothing in particular.

The sun was racing in the morning sky, and like most August days in the South, the temperature was already on the strong side of eighty degrees.

Maggie turned to look at Sam when she heard the back door open. He couldn't get to her quickly enough.

"I see some things haven't changed since high school," Sam observed, half joking.

"I still love being outdoors," Maggie said. "Sam, I want you to leave."

Maggie's command stopped Sam dead in his tracks. He was reduced to stunned silence. He had no defense, no comeback. Was this part of a cruel nightmare? Was he still in Brazil, suffering from the effects of malaria and this was part of a hallucination? No, this was real.

All of a sudden, Sam felt the hot sun beating down on his head. The humidity was playing at his temples. "I don't understand." *That was an understatement,* Sam thought. At least he managed to say something.

"I don't want to talk about it. I just can't do it."

"Is this about last night?"

"No. Last night was my fault. I just can't do this. Please, gather your things and go. Please."

Sam was struggling with his emotions. He wanted to challenge Maggie. One minute, she's climbing into bed next to him, and the next minute, she's asking him to pack his bags. He wanted to try to reason with her, but he could tell she was dead serious. His heart said stay and fight, but his head said retreat. Retreat didn't mean defeat; it just meant he could live to fight another day.

"I'll get my things. Whatever I did, I'm sorry." He figured the fewer the words, the better.

"It's not you, Sam. It's me. I'm the one who needs to apologize. And I am sorry. I didn't mean to give you the wrong idea, but it doesn't change anything. I still want you to leave."

There was nothing left to say. Nothing left for Sam to do but leave Maggie's house, leave Natchitoches, and leave Louisiana. He went inside and packed his bags along with his memories. While he was packing, Sam made another decision. Yes, he had to leave the old Victorian, but he didn't have to leave Natchitoches. He would stay for a day or two, hold his breath. It would give him time to think of another strategy.

Maggie was still sitting in the swing when he went back outside. He couldn't help his feelings, even if she did want him to leave. Maggie was so beautiful sitting in that swing, her hair gently blowing in the summer breeze. He wanted to be mad, but somehow, he couldn't summon the energy. Certainly, he was upset with her decision; his insides were a jumble of nerves, but he couldn't be mad.

"Here is my cell number," Sam began, handing her a card. "I don't have a flight scheduled, so if you could suggest a bed-and-breakfast, I would appreciate it."

"Sure. Try the Queen Anne House. Just ask anyone in

town, and they can give you directions. It was kind of you to come. Believe it or not, I had a wonderful evening."

"That's what my left brain can't figure out, but I'm not going to argue with you. I have to respect your decision. After all, if there's one thing we know for sure in the twenty-first century, it's that 'no' means 'no.'"

"You are such a good guy, and that makes it even tougher for me. You don't come across good guys every day—or even every lifetime."

"It's trite but true, Maggie. Life isn't always fair. Sometimes being a good guy just isn't enough. But, as much as I care about you, I've got to live with myself. I found out the hard way that it's much easier in the long run if you do what's right. I wish I had the right formula—or the secret to your heart."

"Don't ever stop being a good guy. Promise?"

"I'm going to try. Besides, what choice do I have? I can't be anything else with you. You bring out the best in me."

"Give me a hug goodbye," Maggie said, coming toward Sam with her arms open.

Sam wanted to stand there hugging her forever. He closed his eyes and breathed deeply. That was how he wanted to remember her—in his arms surrounded by the warmth of a summer's day. Maggie hugged him back and stayed there as long as she could balance on her tiptoes.

When they let each other go, Sam squeezed her hand one last time and turned to leave without saying a word.

The rental car was your basic Ford Focus, but Sam was glad he opted for the GPS system. He punched in Queen Anne House, Natchitoches, Louisiana, and waited for directions. What did it matter? All he had was time now. He could schedule a flight anytime. Sam had no regrets. He was glad he came to see Maggie. He would always have their one night together.

As Sam followed orders from his GPS, he was able to take in a little more of Natchitoches. It was quaint, for sure. It wasn't Paris, or Venice, or Hong Kong, or Rio de Janeiro. Then again, neither were 99 percent of every city in every country. What it did have was one special person, and that made it even better than Paris in the spring or Rio de Janeiro in January.

The bed-and-breakfast was less than fifteen miles from Maggie's home. There were a few twists and turns, but, thanks to modern technology, Sam didn't have any trouble finding it. For Sam, there was something special about these lovely little inns. Nothing wrong with staying in a Ritz-Carlton, but he much preferred staying in a bed-and-breakfast than in your typical mid-priced hotel, even if it did cost more. The experience was well worth it.

As soon as he walked into the Queen Anne House, Sam

knew he and Maggie shared something else—the same good taste in a bed-and-breakfast. Over the years, Sam had been in well more than a hundred small hotels on several continents. Sometimes he was disappointed, but more often than not, the old homes provided charming accommodations.

In some way, this old home reminded Sam of Maggie's Victorian. The Queen Anne was turn of the century, painted in a light yellow with white trim. The front porch, complete with rocking chairs, was perfect for those spring and summer evenings in the South. The parlor was filled to the brim with antique furniture, including a nineteenth-century couch and chair. A Mac laptop sat on an old desk, which was nestled in one corner of the room.

"Good morning, and welcome to the Queen Anne House." The woman greeting Sam was probably in her midtwenties, and she had short blonde hair and a nice smile.

"Good morning." This was anything but a good morning for Sam. "I was hoping you would have a room for me."

"For how many nights, Mr. ..."

"Mr. Roberts. Sam Roberts. Just one. At least, at this point." Sam was trying to be the optimist.

"We do have rooms available. One minute and let me ask my mom what's still open." The young woman excused herself and went down the hall. In a moment, she returned with her mother.

"Yes, sir, how can we be of service? Please excuse Sally. She's just filling in before she returns to college. She's working on her doctorate in social science. As you can tell, I'm a proud mom, Phyllis Conrad."

"Congratulations," Sam said, turning to Sally. "And congratulations to you, too, Mom. I know you must be proud. I'm looking for a room for one night."

"I think we have the perfect room for you, Mr. Roberts. Just let me get my husband. One more minute." In less than a minute, Mrs. Conrad returned with her husband.

"Mr. Roberts, welcome to our humble home. Please allow me to introduce myself. I'm Paul Conrad. We indeed have the perfect room for you—the Library Room."

"I hope it has a bed and a bath, but I must admit, I do like books," Sam said.

"Yes, well, you will love this room, Mr. Roberts. It is beautifully appointed, with a beautiful king-sized bed and a Jacuzzi bath. You will be very comfortable with us, I promise."

"Sounds great." Sam was ready to get to his room and relax—or at least try to relax.

Sally said, "Please forgive me for gathering the entire family, Mr. Roberts, but I thought you looked familiar.

Mom recognized you, and so did Dad. It's not every day we have a famous person stay at our bed-and-breakfast."

"I'm not as famous as you might think, but I appreciate the thought," Sam said as he took the key.

The room was just as Mr. Conrad had advertised. It was on the first floor, which was a big plus, and the big bay window looking out on the gardens added an air of tranquility. The sitting room was more than Sam needed, but it would be a great place to relax and read. He had brought a couple of books, but the eight-foot walnut bookcase looked like it held several enticing options.

It only took Sam a few minutes to unpack and locate the flat-screen television hidden in the armoire. He always found it ironic that everyone wanted twenty-first-century technology, but they wanted it to fit in a nineteenth-century piece of furniture. No matter. He rarely watched television, but maybe there was a golf tournament that could occupy his mind.

He wasn't hungry, but he knew he better eat something. Just as he was about to raid the minibar tucked in the closet, Sam heard a knock at the door. It was Mrs. Conrad, or, at least, he thought it was Mrs. Conrad. Her head was obscured by a huge gift basket filled with fruit and cheese.

"We are so excited to have such a celebrity at the Queen Anne House," Mrs. Conrad said as she rushed past Sam.

"May I put this on the coffee table in the sitting room?" Before Sam could answer, she placed the basket in the middle of the table.

"This is so kind of you, but it wasn't necessary," Sam said. "Believe me, I'm far from a celebrity."

"You are to us. We are so pleased to have you here, even if it is just for one night. We promise not to tell anyone you are here, but if we could get a photo of you before you go, that would be great. Please forgive me for gushing like this. My husband is a big fan. If you need anything, just let us know. Anything at all." Then Mrs. Conrad was gone as quickly as she appeared.

Over the years, Sam had become accustomed to sports fans fawning over him. It was part of being a sports commentator on a national network, but somehow, it always made him feel uncomfortable.

When he was in South America, few people ever recognized him, much less asked for an autograph or photo op. He knew that celebrity was a fleeting thing. Sam tried to keep everything in perspective; he never asked for his fifteen minutes of fame, and he never wanted to get caught up in the trappings of celebrity.

After he decided to leave the network, he knew that his star would fade, but that was just fine. He understood there was the Sam Roberts sports fans thought they knew and the real Sam Roberts he shared with friends and colleagues.

It was difficult for Sam to ever be upset with fans of his work. His career enabled him to travel the world and be a part of many memorable and breathtaking events. And he was paid handsomely for commenting on sports. Now his fleeting fame had given him another perk—a fruit and cheese basket, including a variety of snack crackers. It was just after noon, and the growling in his midsection told him he had better stop to eat. Sam opened a can of Diet Dr Pepper and took a big drink. He was about to slice an apple and sample some cheese when he heard another knock at the door. What did the Conrads want this time? Perhaps Mrs. Conrad couldn't wait a couple of hours, and she was returning with her camera.

When Sam opened the door, he was excited to see it wasn't Phyllis Conrad.

"Can we talk?" Sam could see that Maggie had been crying.

"Did you come up with another reason we can't be together?" Sam was sorry as soon as the words left his lips.

"I deserve your sarcasm, I know, but just give me a few minutes. Please."

"Sure. We can go into the sitting room," he said, shutting the door behind her. "By the way, you do have good taste. This is a beautiful inn."

"I knew the Queen Anne was nice, but I didn't know the room came with such an elegant fruit and cheese basket." Maggie took a seat on the antique blue velvet couch, which was still in perfect condition.

"It doesn't, but that's another story for another time. Okay, Maggie, I'm listening. Do you mind if I eat a little something? I haven't had anything all day. I bet you haven't eaten either. Can I offer you something? Can I get you something to drink from the minibar?"

"No, I'm fine. I had some coffee and toast early this morning. I want to say what I came here to say while I still have the nerve."

"I'm not so sure this is a good idea. After all, I started this whole thing. If I had never come to your home yesterday, none of this would have happened."

"Can you just be quiet for a moment? Sit and listen."

Before Maggie could continue, there was another knock at Sam's door. Mrs. Conrad was back, and she had her iPhone camera in hand.

"Mrs. Conrad, do you know Maggie McWilliams? I mean Maggie Duncan."

"Yes, I believe we have met. My daughter, Sally, went to high school with your twins."

"Hello, Phyllis. Sure, I remember you. How is Sally?

"She's working for her dad and me before she returns to

the University of Southern California in a couple of weeks," Mrs. Conrad said. "I hear your girls are working in the Peace Corps. I'm glad they are doing well."

Maggie could see the look on Mrs. Conrad's face. "Sam and I are old friends from high school. A hundred years ago. We are just about to catch up on old times."

Mrs. Conrad could also tell that Maggie had been crying. "Everything okay, Maggie?"

"Great. Yes, I'm fine. I promise."

"I know you've been through a difficult time the past couple of years, Maggie."

"Thanks." Even two years later, Maggie still didn't really know what to say in those moments.

"Mr. Roberts, can I shoot a quick photo of you? Do you mind?" Mrs. Conrad asked, turning back to Sam.

He wanted to say that, yes, he did mind, but it was much easier just to shoot the photo and be done with it.

"Paul, come on in. Mr. Roberts said we could take a photo. Maggie, would you mind?"

Since he was by far the tallest, Sam put Mr. and Mrs. Conrad on either side of him. He had done this a thousand times, so it was routine for him.

Maggie took the iPhone, turned on the flash, told everyone to smile, counted to three, and hit the button.

She shot a couple of extra photos to make sure she had a good one.

"We are so sorry to disturb you," Mrs. Conrad said, shoving her husband toward the door. "We promise to give you your privacy. Again, welcome to the Queen Anne House."

Maggie knew exactly where she had left off. "You have no idea how hard this is for me. You show up at my door, faint, and profess your feelings for me. It was all so much for me, and so flattering."

"I didn't mean to overwhelm you, Maggie. I wanted to see you and find out what was happening in your life. I will admit I had an ulterior motive, but I wasn't going to put you in a situation you would regret. Or that I would regret."

"I know I'm giving you mixed signals."

"Now, that was the understatement of the year."

"I know it was crazy climbing into bed with you last night. It was an impulse, and it was the scariest thing I've ever done in my life."

"You are now officially the first woman to ever go to bed with me and then say it was the scariest thing you ever did." Sam couldn't help but get in a little jab.

"I didn't mean it that way. I'm more vulnerable than I thought. So many things have been going through my head. I'm a grown woman, and I take responsibility for what I did, but it really was scary for me. It has been so long since I've been intimate with anyone. I miss being close to someone."

"What are you really thinking, Maggie?"

"For instance, Sam, we don't have anything in common. You live in a jungle; I live in this small town in Louisiana. And when you aren't living in a jungle, you travel the world signing autographs and collecting fruit and cheese baskets."

"You have to have a better excuse than that," Sam said.

"You've never been married, and I have. You don't have any children, and I do. It's been forty years since we've been around each other. We really don't know each other at all. Not really."

"I asked you last night if you were sure of what you were doing," Sam said. "Remember? I wish I had just told you to sleep in your own bed, but I was selfish. I wanted to be close to you."

"You are overanalyzing this," Maggie said. "What we did or didn't do in bed has nothing to do with my feelings."

"I'm here, and I have all day to listen," Sam said. "Explain away."

Maggie took a deep breath, sat straight on the couch, and folded her legs beneath her.

"There are so many places I could begin, Sam, and that is the problem."

"Pick one, please. We'll make a list of the pluses and minuses."

"My children. What would they say? It's only been two years since their father died. It would take too much time and energy to convince them I want another man in my life—in their lives. They have never even met you."

"Have you had any kind of conversation with Lucy and Lily about your future?"

"I'm glad you said their names. That tells me you think of them as real individuals, even if you haven't met them. To answer your question, sure, we talk in general. How are you, Mom? Everything okay with you, Mom? The usual conversations children have with parents. Nothing deep."

"Please don't take offense, but it sounds like they have moved on with their lives. Didn't you say they are volunteering in Thailand?

"You don't have children, Sam, and I don't mean that in a bad way, but children always go their own way. I must admit I've spoiled them, but they are such good kids. They want me to be happy, but they want me to be happy within their universe."

"I can't help the fact that I don't have children, but I think I know human nature. How about this: What if you ask them what they think? I'm not going to come between you and your children. I do understand enough about relationships to know that I'll always know my place when it comes to you and your daughters."

"I talk with them every week—on Sunday mornings before I go to Mass. I guess I could ask them, but I'm not sure they are ready for me to have another man in my life."

"You won't know until you ask, will you?" Sam got up from the couch and walked to the huge bay window that looked out on the garden. "How would you feel about going into the garden and getting some fresh air and a little sunshine? Those huge trees will give us plenty of shade. What do you say?"

Maggie nodded.

"Would you like a drink from my fabulous minibar?"

"Water would be great."

"No problem. You sure you don't want any fruit or cheese?"

"I'm fine, thanks."

Sam led the way and found an old, wooden park bench beneath a tall maple tree. The bench was still in great shape and was fairly comfortable. "How about this spot, Maggie? There's even a little breeze today."

"It is lovely out here," she said, taking a big sip of water.

It is lovely, but not as lovely as the woman sitting across from me, Sam thought. Her eyes were a light chocolate, but they still shimmered in the afternoon sun. He couldn't imagine a more beautiful woman in the world. "Where were we?" Sam said. "Oh, yes, we were listing the pluses and minuses of us being together."

"Here is minus number two. I don't know if I'm ready for another relationship. I thought I was making some progress after David's death, and then you came to my door." Maggie could see a little twitch in Sam's mouth when she said those words. "No, Sam. It wasn't a bad thing that you found me. It was good, but it was different. You are making me think about David, my life, and what's next for me. In the past few hours, I had to come to the realization that I stuffed a lot of my feelings and my beliefs down deep inside. I put them in some invisible vault so I wouldn't have to deal with anything. I just went about my life, staying in my routine. It was my way of coping."

"Maggie, I understand what you are saying, but at some point, you have to move forward with your life."

"I'm scared of having another marriage end badly."

"You mean David dying?"

"That's only half of it, Sam. You have no idea—or at least I don't think you have any idea of what really happened with David and me."

"I'm here, and it's a stunning afternoon."

"I'm not ready to go there right now, but I want to talk about us for a minute."

"My favorite subject."

"Tell me again why you love me. Or why you think you love me."

"It began with our first conversation. It's insane, I know, and it's hard to explain. Something clicked for me the first time we talked. Then, it wasn't long before we met. Double click. Then, we began to date. My feelings grew. I just loved you more each day."

"You knew at eighteen that you wanted to spend the rest of your life with me?"

"It's not as crazy as it sounds. A lot of married couples dated in high school. Okay, maybe not a lot, but enough. And they get married. And if it's a good marriage, they have a wonderful life. I was lucky. I found the person for me early in life. It was you, Maggie."

"How lucky could it be if you've been single for forty years?"

"Don't feel sorry for me. I'm a grown man. I make my own decisions. There is nothing wrong with being single. In our society, there is a stigma attached to single people. Somehow, we believe we are only fulfilled through marriage. Being single is a lifestyle. In fact, I bet I could go to downtown Natchitoches and ask twenty men if they would like to trade places with me—and 70 percent of them would say yes."

"Sure, look at your career."

"I'm not talking about my career. I'm just talking about being single. Remember, half of the marriages in this country end in divorce. I never wanted to be divorced. So I waited until the right person came along. Honestly, I'm open to finding that person. I've always believed it was you. Still do, but if this doesn't work out, I'll go back to my life and see what happens. If someone comes along and knocks me off my feet, then I'll marry her. If not, then that's fine, too. I've had a terrific life. I believe it would be better with you, Maggie."

"It sounds like you've put a lot of thought into this."

"Forty years. When we left for college, I gave you the benefit of the doubt. I told myself that you were right and that we should date other people. Enjoy ourselves. If it was meant to be, if we were meant to be together, it would happen. After all, you were on one coast, and I was on the other."

Maggie took another long drink of water. "I have a confession to make, Sam."

"We are both Catholic, so I guess that's appropriate."

"My father is the one who insisted that I break it off with you. When you are eighteen, you obey your parents. I didn't argue with my dad. It wouldn't have done any good. I don't know why I would even bring that up now. Both Mom and

Dad passed away about twelve years ago. I just wanted you to know. It's the honest truth."

"That makes me feel better, but there's no reason to go there now. You have two great kids, and I've had a fabulous career with memories I will cherish forever. I am a little confused about why we can't look to our future."

"I can't stand the thought of another failed marriage. Or, heaven forbid, what if you die? I don't know if I could go through that again. I know I'm not making much sense."

"It's better to talk about all of this now. I want to clear the air so we can fix this. You have my head spinning. One minute, you are climbing into bed with me—and the next minute, you ask me to leave your house. An hour after you kick me to the curb, you find me and want to talk. Would it be best if I leave Natchitoches and give you time to think? As you know, I'm a patient person. I've waited forty years; I can wait a little longer."

"All I know is that I want to keep talking and see where it takes us. All right?"

"Deal."

"You really are a good guy, aren't you, Sam?"

"I try to be nice, but that's the problem. Sometimes I wish I could be that macho guy who uses women and moves on to the next one. Women like the bad boys, don't they?"

"Not me. That's why I have to believe you are a good

guy, Sam. That's why I got into my car and drove over here like a bat out of Hades to find you. I'm just so mixed up, and giving you mixed signals doesn't help matters. I don't know what I'm saying."

It was time to take another chance. Sam took Maggie's hand and brought her to her feet. He put his arms around her, closed his eyes, and drew her close. He squeezed so hard he wondered if she could breathe. He could smell the hint of a gardenia bush, and it reminded him of a perfume Maggie had worn so long ago.

Maggie pulled back for a moment to look up into Sam's eyes. At six feet two inches, Sam was a good half-a-foot taller. Maggie stood on her toes, brushed her lips against his, and then pressed harder.

Another pleasant surprise. She tastes so sweet, Sam thought.

"That's what I've been trying to tell you, Sam," she said, still wrapped in his arms.

"I think I understand, but not completely. I think I need another lesson."

"No problem. All those years in the classroom taught me that repetition is the best way to learn." Maggie kissed him hard once again, putting her hands on his cheeks and then brushing his hair. She could feel her heart flutter and tiny goose bumps rise on her arms.

"You are a good teacher," he said, his head still reeling

with a million thoughts. "I've got an idea. Why don't we go on a date? Do you have dinner plans tonight?"

"I just happen to be free this evening. It's been a very long time since I've had a date. I think a date at my age would be lovely."

"Since I don't know much about your city, can you make reservations for seven thirty? I'll come by for you later."

"How about this? Not only will I make reservations, I'll come back to the Queen Anne House, and we can leave from here. I know exactly where I want to have dinner, and this is on the way. It's our best restaurant and my favorite. The owner is a friend of mine, and I know he will have a table for us."

"See? We have even more in common." Sam took Maggie by the hand and led her back into his room. "I love great restaurants and great cuisine."

"I better go. I have a lot to do. I only have a couple of hours before I see you again."

Sam gave Maggie a goodbye hug, but he decided not to squeeze so hard this time. He wanted her alive and well for dinner. By the grace of God, he had new life with Maggie. He didn't know what would happen next, but he knew he was going to make the most of it.

Chapter 3

"Sam Roberts, is that really you?" The words came bounding across the dining room. Maggie knew the voice was familiar, but she was puzzled when she saw the owner of the Landing racing toward their table. How could her good friend know Sam? After all, Kent Gresham had been in the restaurant business for most of his adult life, and as far as Maggie knew, he had always lived in Natchitoches. And for the past twenty-something years, he had owned and operated the Landing, one of the best seafood and steak restaurants in northwest Louisiana.

"Is that really you, Mr. Roberts? Dining in my humble restaurant?" Kent Gresham was acting more like a starstruck teenager than one of the greatest chefs in Louisiana.

"Please, just call me Sam."

"Kent Gresham." He started shaking Sam's hand like he was pumping for oil. "Welcome to the Landing."

"I'm glad my friend suggested we dine here this evening," Sam said.

"It's such a pleasure to meet you in person," Kent continued. "I've seen you so much on TV that I think I know you. I'm a big fan … was a big fan … am a big fan."

"You are too kind, but I've been retired for a couple of years now." Sam wanted to move this along, but he knew from experience that it was better to be polite. Besides, everyone who wanted to greet him meant well. Sam always tried to keep his celebrity, if you could call it that, in perspective.

"I know, but we still miss you, Mr. Roberts … Sam. I speak for every sports fan in America when I say we all miss you. Could I ask for an autograph or have my photo taken with you?"

"No problem. Whatever I can do for you."

"Aren't you going to say hello to your most loyal customer?" Maggie asked, wedging her words between the two men shaking hands. She had been ignored long enough.

"I'm sorry. Please forgive me, Maggie," Kent said, "but it's not every day we get a national celebrity in our restaurant. Excuse me for one minute." The restaurant owner was true to his word. He was back in a couple of minutes. "This is my wife, Sam."

"Maria Gresham," she said, using her apron to clean

the lens on the Nikon point-and-shoot in her hands. By now, almost the entire restaurant was looking at Sam and Maggie. "My husband is a big fan. Please come back to the network. All I hear is how much Kent misses you."

"Hello, Maria," Maggie said in a subdued tone.

Maria said, "Maggie, I didn't know you knew Sam Roberts."

"Why didn't you tell us?" Kent asked.

"Obviously, I'm the only one who doesn't know my friend is a celebrity," Maggie said, looking at Sam.

"Celebrity is way overrated," Sam said.

"You were only the very best sports analyst on television," Kent said. "No matter the sport—football, basketball, baseball, golf, tennis, the Olympics—no one was even a close second."

"And believe me," Maria said, "my husband watches every sport, every night. To Kent, Sam Roberts is a god."

"You are too kind, Mr. and Mrs. Gresham." Sam had always been good with names. "Thank you."

"Why don't I take a photo of you, Sam, with Kent and Maria?" Maggie offered.

"Would you please? That would be so kind. Maria, give the camera to Maggie," Kent said.

Sam stood beside the table with Kent on one side and

Maria on the other. The three of them standing together looked like a roller-coaster graph of the stock market.

Sam said, "How about if I sit in my chair, and the two of you can stand on either side of me?"

Kent and Maria obeyed as if the order had come from on high.

"Okay, everyone," Maggie said, making sure everyone was in the frame. "On three. One. Two. Three." Sam could tell Maggie had taken a few photos in her time; she probably had a million or so of her twins. "One or two more, just in case. Smile."

"Everything is on me tonight," Kent said, retrieving the camera from Maggie and giving it to his wife.

"No, we couldn't," Sam said.

"No arguments, Mr. Roberts. Sam. My pleasure."

"Kent is a stubborn man, Sam," Maggie said. "You better take him up on his offer—or he will be insulted."

"You know me very well, Maggie," Kent said. "Again, let me offer my apology. I didn't mean to ignore you. You are a beautiful person inside and out."

"That's exactly what I've been trying to tell her," Sam said.

"I'll forgive you this time, Kent, if you have my favorite entree on the menu." Maggie was partial to the Gunpowder

Salmon. The name of the dish caught Sam's attention because it didn't exactly sound appetizing.

"No problem, Maggie. The Gunpowder Salmon is on the menu this evening. Mr. Roberts, I promise my salmon has a wonderful taste." Kent could see that Sam was a little skeptical. "Now, I promise to leave you two alone. Come back and see us soon, Mr. Roberts. You are always welcome here."

Kent scurried to the kitchen and returned with two menus and a bottle of Kendall-Jackson chardonnay. He also subtly placed a blank sheet of paper on the table for Sam's autograph.

"If you like, you can give Maggie a copy of the photo, and I'll sign it," Sam offered. He had an ulterior motive. Even if it didn't work out with Maggie, it would give him one more chance to talk with her.

"Bless you, Sam. That would be wonderful." Kent was gushing. "Now I'm going to disappear into the kitchen to make preparations for your special evening." In a blink, Kent was gone.

"Wow, I didn't know you were such a big deal, Sam. You should have brought your sunglasses so no one would recognize you. If this continues, you can hire me as your professional photographer."

"Time out." Sam was beginning to feel uncomfortable. "How about we hit the reset button."

"What does that mean?" Maggie asked, sensing a little frustration in Sam's voice.

"Can we pretend this is our first date and start fresh? I know we have a history, but can we give it a try?"

"Deal."

"What's your favorite color?" Sam couldn't resist.

"We are starting from the beginning, aren't we? Green. And you? What's your favorite color."

"I'm in my blue phase. And your favorite movie?" Sam decided he would just go down the list of favorite things.

Maggie didn't hesitate before saying, "*Pretty Woman.*"

"In that case, we can leave now," Sam joked.

"Since we haven't had our food yet, how about I try again? Would you believe *Titanic*?"

"Okay, I'll give you that one. I'll go with *An Affair to Remember.*"

"I guess we are sentimental, aren't we, Sam?"

"Favorite song?"

"I can't believe you actually asked that question, Sam Roberts. You should know better."

"It's still the same—even forty years later?"

"Still the same."

"How about dancing? Do you still like to go dancing?"

Even as he was asking the question, Sam regretted his words. Thankfully, it didn't seem to bother Maggie.

"It's been ages, but I do like to dance. Weddings are about the only opportunity I get to dance, and I haven't been to a wedding in I don't know how long."

Sam never forgot the first time he danced with Maggie. Two teenagers thinking they were adults. Two kids believing they were the most sophisticated eighteen-year-olds in the world, much less at the country club in Beaumont, Texas.

During that first dance, Sam marveled at Maggie's beauty. Her hair was in a French twist that would make Audrey Hepburn jealous. Maggie's red satin gown accentuated the sparkle in her deep brown eyes.

Sam thought Maggie was sweet and kind, funny and genuine. They were still dancing when the band finished the last song of the evening. Sam wanted one more minute to hold Maggie close. One more minute to close his eyes and drink in her smell. His love for Maggie was confirmed and affirmed that evening. This was the woman he would marry. He was sure of it. This was the woman he would be with for the rest of his life. He didn't tell anyone because he knew what they would say.

How can a teenager all of eighteen years old absolutely

know he is in love? After all, love can be a complicated matter. How did Sam know he wouldn't meet his soul mate in college or on his first job? Maybe his soul mate lived in Korea or Australia or Scotland.

All legitimate questions, but Sam always had the same answer—Maggie was different. He just knew. At worst, he had bad timing. If he lived in the Middle Ages, falling in love at eighteen wouldn't be any big deal. Even getting married would have been a breeze.

That summer with Maggie was the best ninety days of his life. He spent as much time as he could with her, going for long walks, talking about saving the world. There's no better feeling than knowing that, for the first time, someone is occupying your every waking thought.

Sam never felt so good about life—and he never felt so horrible when it all came crashing down just before he and Maggie left for college.

"Can I offer you an appetizer this evening while you are waiting on your entrees?" The young waitress standing over Maggie and Sam broke his train of thought. "Perhaps some fried green tomatoes or pan-roasted clams?"

Maggie and Sam shook their heads at the same time.

"Are you sure? Chef Kent said you are a special couple."

Maggie said, "It all sounds so delicious, but if I know the chef, we will have more than we could ever eat at one meal. Sam, you really should try the gumbo."

"Seafood or alligator sausage?" the waitress asked.

"I better stick with seafood—no offense to the gators," Sam said.

"I'll have a Caesar salad please," Maggie added.

"It would be my pleasure." The waitress scurried to the kitchen.

"I don't see salmon on the menu," Sam said.

"Chef saves it for his best customers," Maggie said. "Tonight, thanks to you, I guess we qualify."

"I think you have a little something to do with it, Maggie. I saw that twinkle in his eye when he greeted you."

"We do go back a long way. I can't believe I've been in Natchitoches all these years. I love my job at the university, and I love the quaint feel of this city."

Sam didn't know much about Natchitoches, although he frequently would get it confused with Nacogdoches in Texas. He did remember Natchitoches was one of the oldest cities, if not the oldest city, west of the Mississippi River. Perhaps he would get a chance to see a little more of it before he left, although deep inside, he hoped he would never leave.

"Now, where were we?" Sam asked, getting the

conversation back to his favorite subject: Maggie. "What is the meaning of life, Maggie?"

Maggie couldn't help but laugh out loud. "I thought we were going to keep this light and breezy? After all, it is our first date, right?"

"By the way, are we going Dutch tonight?" Sam teased as the waitress brought their first course.

"I think it's your turn to buy," Maggie said without hesitation. "Don't forget—I fed you last night."

Sam had to admit the gumbo was the best he had ever tasted. When you eat gumbo, it's all about the roux. Sam had never made gumbo, but he knew that making roux was not easy. Chef Kent did a very good job, and Sam was impressed. Maggie's Caesar salad looked fresh and wonderful, as well.

"How's the salad?"

"I like that question better than asking me the meaning of life. My Caesar is great."

The evening went as Sam had planned—or as well as any first date could have gone. Their conversation was as fresh as the grilled salmon, which had just the right amount of salt, pepper, and garlic seasoning. Dessert—bread pudding that could have fed a table of eight—was too much, but Sam and Maggie managed a polite bite or two.

"If you don't mind, I'm going to the kitchen to fight with

our chef over the bill and congratulate him on our wonderful meal," Sam said. "Would you like to come with me?"

"You go, Sam. I don't want to fight over another bill. Kent is just too generous."

Maggie didn't expect Sam to be gone so long. It was only fifteen minutes, but when you are waiting, fifteen minutes can seem like fifteen hours.

Maggie said, "Sam, thanks for a great time, but we can't pretend any longer. When we get back to my house, we have to have a serious talk. Your delaying tactic was artfully done tonight, but you have to listen to what I have to say."

All the way back to Maggie's house, not a word was said. Sam was grateful for the smooth jazz station on the radio. He had no idea what Maggie was about to say, but he knew one thing: the words "I do" weren't going to be part of the conversation.

Chapter 4

"You are a good guy, Sam, and I owe you the truth." Maggie could feel her hands tremble. "It's not fair for me to tell you to leave without an explanation."

Maggie certainly had Sam's attention. He took a sip of water and settled into the captain's chair in the Victorian's living room, half listening, half planning his defense.

"I'm going to give you all the reasons we can't be together," Maggie said. She sounded like a prosecuting attorney laying out her case.

"I can give you one reason we should be together," Sam shot back.

"Please don't interrupt, Sam. This is hard enough for me." Maggie crossed her legs on her off-white couch, staring straight at Sam. "I'm going to start at the very beginning, all those years ago. We only had one summer together, Sam, but it was amazing. I was far from an adult, but I was in love. In love with you. Everything we did together—going to a movie, going for a bike ride, going for a pizza—was perfect. The only other thing I loved was dancing."

That comment brought a smile to Sam's face. He remembered buying a ticket to watch Maggie dance. He had saved that program for years. It probably was still buried in an old trunk somewhere in his parents' old home. He would never forget seeing her name in bold type: Maggie McWilliams, principal dancer. And he would never forget watching as she glided effortlessly across the stage, from pirouette to plié. Beautiful, graceful, confident.

"Do you remember when I told you I didn't want to see you anymore?"

Boy, did Sam remember. He could only nod.

"Well, I wanted to keep seeing you—even though we were going to different colleges. My father told me I needed to end it. I didn't have the courage to tell him no, and I didn't have the courage to tell you the truth. He just saw you as an athlete who would be a coach someday. Dad didn't think you would amount to much."

Looking back and being objective, Sam had to admit her father was probably right. He thought perhaps he could play professional sports or be a coach if all else failed. Going into broadcasting was a lucky break.

"You went about your life, and I went about my life.

David came along, and we fell in love and married. He was working toward a doctorate in psychology, and I was working toward a doctorate in social science. It just made sense."

"I was hurt and immature," Sam said. "That's what eighteen-year-old kids do. If you didn't want me, I wasn't going to come begging. Besides, I had to work hard to keep my scholarship and my grades. I wanted to make the most of my opportunity."

"Life happens while we make plans, right, Sam?"

"Forty years of life."

"Eventually, we moved to Natchitoches. I'm a tenured professor at Northwestern State University. David opened his practice and immediately began to see patients. We've been here ... I've been here more than twenty-five years. We were happy. We raised the twins in this house and celebrated anniversaries, birthdays, all those special moments married couples share. It wasn't the best marriage ever, but it was a good marriage. Solid. Comfortable. At least, until two years ago."

"You don't have to talk about David if you don't feel like it."

"I need to talk about David. I have to tell you about David. It's important. One day, David came home from his family therapy practice and told me he was in trouble. I had never seen him so distraught. I knew it was serious."

That day would forever be seared into Maggie's mind. It was a Thursday, just after five in the afternoon, and David came to the kitchen where she was heating leftover lasagna. It was odd, but Maggie remembered David was wearing a baby blue polo shirt—her favorite.

David asked her to put their meal on hold. He had to talk. They went to the dining table, which was just off the kitchen. Maggie could see a tear come to his eye. David began to tell her about one of his patients, a teenager, which was really strange because David never talked about any of his patients, especially in specific terms.

Her name was Coco Conners. She was fourteen years old, and she was a freshman at the local high school. Coco's mom had sent her to David because she was acting out at school, and her grades were on a downward spiral. It didn't take David long to diagnose the problem. He had seen it a thousand times. The Conners were going through a nasty divorce, and Coco was caught between the two parents she loved. It was complicated by the fact that Coco's dad decided to accept a promotion and move to the East Coast.

The more David met with Coco, the more he could see her potential. He could tell she was special in many ways. First, she was smart and clever for her age. Secondly, she was gorgeous, with short-cropped blonde hair, icy blue eyes, and lips as red as any sunset.

David was meeting with Coco once a week. Then he increased it to twice a week—not because she needed the extra counseling session—he just wanted to see her. Intellectually, he knew he was treading in dangerous territory, but he couldn't help himself. In his midfifties, he was going through a midlife crisis. He wanted to be young again, and Coco was his chance.

It was a disaster waiting to happen because Coco was looking for a father figure, and she found one in David. It wasn't too long before David and Coco were having sex on his couch. Instead of working through problems, David was creating problems. He should have known this wasn't going to be some discreet fling. This was a fourteen-year-old kid, but he didn't care if things ended badly. David was enjoying the moment. He was desirable and young again.

Then everything blew up in his face. Coco wanted to marry him—or at the very least to be with him. She wanted them to run away to anywhere and begin a new life. When David told her that would be impossible, she went ballistic. If David wouldn't run away with her, Coco warned, she would tell her mom and then go to the police. After all, she was only fourteen.

David decided to call her bluff. He tried to calm her

down, but he didn't have much luck. He said they would talk about it again at their next session. Coco didn't wait until their next session. She was mad, and she wanted revenge. She kept her word. After she told her mom the story, they went straight to the police. It wasn't long before a detective was in David's office asking questions and asking him to come down to the station. He said he had to go home first.

"That's when he told me the story," Maggie said. "It was like a nightmare. It was—I hate to say it—crazy. It was surreal. After David finished, he told me he loved me, and then he left. I thought he was going to the police station, but he went back to his office—and hung himself."

"Maggie ..."

"Very few people know all the details. I didn't tell you this story, Sam, to shock you. I didn't tell you so you would feel sorry for me. I told you so you can know why I don't trust men anymore. I thought I knew this man. We had been married our entire adult lives. It's been two years, and it's still difficult for me. You can imagine how it affected the twins."

Sam listened patiently and attentively. When she was finished, he moved to the couch and took Maggie's hand in his, sitting next to her in silence. Sam felt horrible, but he wasn't going to tell Maggie. Not now. Not ever. He wasn't going to tell Maggie he had kept up with her from afar.

He didn't want her to think of him as a stalker. There were many times over those years that he hoped Maggie and David would get a divorce. Occasionally, Sam even prayed, that David would die.

"So that's one big reason I can't be with you," Maggie said. "I'm scared, and I'm scarred. In some ways, I blame myself for David's death."

"You know you aren't to blame, right?"

"I know. That's what I tell myself. I know that in my mind. My priest tells me it's not my fault, my family tells me that it's not my fault, and my friends tell me that it's not my fault. I've got to believe. I have many more good days than bad days, but there is still this tiny voice inside me that won't completely go away."

"No one is perfect."

"Least of all me, but I don't want you to think I'm a basket case. I am getting better. I'm going to continue to work on my life, to work on myself, to know myself better and better, and to try to become a better person."

"What you just described is this process we call life, Maggie. We all go through stages in life. Sometimes we take two steps forward and one step back. Sometimes we take one step forward and two steps back. Maggie, to be honest, there are times I feel I haven't taken a step forward in years, and that is the worst feeling. That means I'm stagnant, and I hate that feeling. Trust me, it's better to be inching forward than going nowhere at all."

"I have two other good reasons to send you packing," Maggie said.

There's more?

"The second issue is my family, and my third issue is you, Sam."

"Forget me for a moment—what about Lily and Lucy?"

"I don't know how they would react to me being with someone else on a full-time basis."

Sam could see it was hard for Maggie to actually say the word *marriage.*

"They haven't even seen me with a man on a part-time basis. I think it would shock them. Their father's death was so traumatic that they signed up for the Peace Corps so they could get out of the country—much less out of this city and state."

"I think you might be surprised." Sam wasn't sure he was right, but he at least wanted to make his case.

"How so?"

"For all practical purposes, they are adults. They know how the world works. I cannot believe they wouldn't want you to be happy. Besides, you are a young woman. Lily and Lucy have to think that sooner or later you would meet someone else, date, maybe even marry again. It just makes good sense."

"I'm not sure it makes sense to them—or me. The twins can be a little contradictory at times. On one hand, they worry about me being alone. They want to know if I am lonely. They also know that, for better or worse, David was their father. No matter what he did, he is still their father. They see us as man and wife. I could be wrong, but I don't think they visualize me with anyone else."

"Like I said, they might fool you. I don't know them, but I'll bet you one scoop of chocolate ice cream they would be accepting of someone you truly love."

"I sound so negative, don't I?"

"You sound like an intelligent, caring, loving person who is trying to figure out the next phase of her life. You don't want to make any bad decisions, especially any bad decisions that affect your family for the rest of your lives."

"I couldn't have said it better myself," Maggie said. "And I could have saved all the money I spent telling my therapist the same thing."

"I believe in therapy, so I would say that was money well spent. In fact, I generally don't trust anyone who doesn't have two therapists on call at all times."

Maggie couldn't help but smile.

"I like that smile. Look at it this way, Maggie. We

communicate very well, although I don't always like what I'm hearing. We are open and honest. Both of us listen. We care. That's what I'm trying to say to you. We have something special here."

"That's why I'm opening up to you, Sam. I want to believe there is something between us, but I just want to make sure of what I'm doing. I need you to be my friend."

"I would think we still are in the friendship stage, especially after last night."

"Sam, we almost went past the friendship stage—thanks to my impulsive behavior."

"I'm glad you were impulsive, but I didn't get the sense you were ready for something more. You are working through a great tragedy in your life. You have children. If I wanted to, I could make a strong argument that we shouldn't be together."

"Like what?"

"Why would I want to dive headfirst into a family situation where there's bound to be complications sooner or later? Not to mention what happened to David."

"When you put it that way, it's pretty convincing. Then, why do you want to be with me?"

"Because I'm crazy about you, or maybe I'm just crazy. Because I love you. Always have, always will." Sam wanted Maggie to see that he could be just as vulnerable. "Whatever the situation, we can work through it. You have been through a bad time in your life, but I want to help you by being there for you. I want to be involved with Lily and Lucy because of what I feel for you. I want to be a part of your family. I'll never have children of my own. I want grandchildren, although I'm well aware I have no vote."

"If it were only that easy," Maggie said.

"Anything worth having is worth the struggle to get it. I know I'll have to earn your children's respect to be a part of your life and their lives. I know I won't automatically pass go and collect two hundred dollars. I'm willing to be patient and pay my dues. You know the old saying 'seeing is believing,' and when they see us together, they will know their mom is happy."

"I need some time to think about all this. I don't have to decide right now, do I?"

"Like I said, take your time. I want you to be sure. Look how many years I've waited. I can wait a while longer. My feelings aren't going to change."

"Thanks for understanding. You are one of the great guys in this world."

"You said there were two things you wanted to discuss."

"Yes. It's about being one of the greatest guys in the world. My mother taught me to never trust a man. I never thought she was right until David had an affair with a fourteen-year-old kid and committed suicide. I thought I knew my husband. Obviously, it was horrible for David, but it also was horrible for me and the girls. Now you are here, and here is the problem I'm having. I'm hearing my mother's voice saying, 'Never trust a man.' You seem so perfect—too perfect—and that reminds me of something my father said: 'If something seems too good to be true, it probably is.'"

"I am far from perfect, Maggie. I'm just a man. If it makes you feel any better, I was engaged one time. It was years ago. She was smart, great career, attractive. The whole package. We dated for a couple of years and then planned this big wedding. That took another eighteen months. One week before the wedding, I called it off. So, if you need a reference on how bad a guy I can be, I can give you one. I think I would be shot if I went anywhere near that family again."

"Why did you call it off?"

"She told me she would rather be divorced than call off the wedding, but I just had to admit I didn't love her enough to spend the rest of my life with her. There is no doubt I should have been more honest with myself and with her. I felt terrible, but I couldn't do it."

"I'll admit that was pretty bad, but if that is the worst thing you've done, then you still are in the almost-perfect category."

"Maggie, you've put me in a horrible position. I now

have to convince you I'm a tragically flawed person. I don't know what to say."

"Don't say anything. We've talked enough for one night."

"How about this. Tomorrow is Sunday. You told me you talk with Lily and Lucy every Sunday morning. How about I come over—and you can introduce me? I can meet them. See what they say about me, about us. Maybe we can go to church together."

After a few moments, Maggie said, "I'll talk to them for a minute and see if they want to meet you. You wait outside, and if they do want to see this new man in my life, I'll come out and get you. Would that be acceptable?"

"Whatever you say, Maggie. I'm playing by your rules."

"If they don't want to meet you, then that will speak volumes."

"Deal. I'm going back to the Queen Anne to get some sleep. I'll see you in the morning. I'll be here at nine sharp."

"We have a lot to think about, Sam. My head is swimming right now."

As Maggie stood, Sam took her in his arms. He gently kissed her, and to his surprise, she pressed her lips against his.

"That was a great kiss for a first date," Sam said, taking Maggie by the hand and walking toward the front door. Sam made a pledge to himself: *It might have been our first date, but it will not be our last one.*

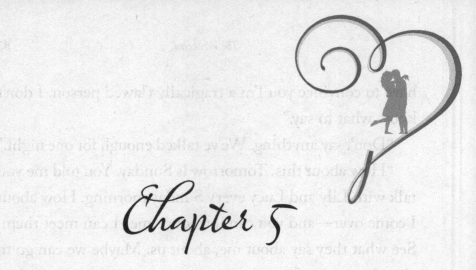

Chapter 5

As he crawled under the covers, Sam knew the next ten hours would feel more like twenty. His king-sized bed in the Library Room was more than comfortable, especially compared to his tiny room and single bed at the mission house in Brazil.

It wouldn't be the first time he had a sleepless night, and it would probably not be the last. Even when he knew sleep would be a distant friend, he lay in bed engulfed in dark. Why didn't he just get up and watch television until he felt sleepy? Why didn't he read a book until he couldn't keep his eyes open any longer? After all, he was staying in the Library Room. He was tired, but he was not sleepy. He just wished he could get his mind from racing ninety miles per hour.

Inevitably, he would think back to the fifth grade at St. Mary's Catholic School and his days on the basketball team. Sam was something of a phenomenon back then. He was in the fifth grade, but he started on the eighth grade team. No one had done it before, and no one had done it since. Unfortunately, Sam never grew another inch after the eighth grade. He was good—good enough to get a scholarship to play in college—but he was not good enough to take his game to the ultimate level.

The memory that almost always came to him in these sleepless moments was death. The father of one of his teammates died during basketball season. Like most fifth graders, Sam had never experienced death. No one in his family had passed away. This was a new experience, a little confusing and a little sad.

Sam's teammate, Nicky, was gone for most of the week. When Nicky returned to the team, he was upbeat, joking, and ready to practice. It seemed so odd to Sam. After all, if your dad dies, shouldn't you be sad? Shouldn't it be one of the worst things that could happen to a kid? To Sam, it just didn't seem like a time to be cutting up and joking with your friends.

After practice one day, Sam asked the coach for a few minutes of his time. Sam asked the coach what was going on with Nicky.

"What do you mean?" coach asked.

"Well, his dad died, and Nicky is joking around like nothing happened. Shouldn't he be more upset?"

"Sit down, Sam, and let me tell you something." Sam could tell his coach was in full teaching mode. "Nicky may seem to be all right, but he's just being strong in front of you guys. You know he's sad and heartbroken. Anyone would be to lose his dad. You have to remember, Sam, Nicky goes home every night, gets into bed, and turns out the lights. When those lights go out, he probably cries himself to sleep every night."

Sam never forgot his coach's words. When the lights go out, it's just you and the dark. You can't hide from your feelings, and you can't hide from what is true and not true. Maybe that's really why Sam got into bed and turned out the lights in these situations. He wanted to know what was real and what was not real. He was looking for the truth.

He had to smile a little, thinking about Maggie calling him perfect. He was so far from perfect that he couldn't stand it. If she only knew the whole truth. Sam had given Maggie a glimpse of his world when he confessed he had been engaged and had walked away a week before the wedding. If she really analyzed what Sam had said, she would figure out just how insensitive he had been in those days.

Sam wasn't wrong to call off the wedding. After all, you shouldn't marry someone you don't love. You shouldn't commit to someone if you don't think you could be with them for your entire life. There's a reason they say, "Until death do us part."

Deep down, Sam knew it wasn't going to work. He knew that he didn't love Jill with his whole being. No, the sin wasn't walking away at the last minute. The sin was getting engaged in the first place.

Sam could have given Maggie more exhibits to prove he was a mere mortal, but it would have served no purpose. Every couple comes into a relationship with some baggage. It's always a question of how much to share. In Sam's experience, too much information about your past only serves to poison the bond you are trying to build as your relationship grows.

Jill was a perfect example. When Sam was away covering World Cup soccer, Jill was staying at his loft in Bristol, Connecticut, for a few days. Sam lived only a couple of blocks from Jill's office, and she could walk to work, which saved time and taxi fare. She stayed over at Sam's every now and then anyway, but only when Sam was at home. This was a first. She and Sam had been dating for about six months, and everything was going like clockwork—until Jill decided to go through Sam's things and play private detective.

Sam hadn't given Jill any reason to be suspicious. She

was alone, and the urge to snoop was overwhelming. Sure enough, she found three journals tucked in the back of Sam's closet. By the time she finished the third journal, Jill knew that Sam had another woman in his life—someone named Maggie.

When Sam returned, it didn't take Jill long to confess to finding and reading the journals. She knew Sam would be mad as a hornet's nest because she had crossed a sacred boundary. She didn't care how mad he would get. She knew she would never be allowed to stay in his apartment alone again. She understood that Sam might even break it off, but Jill didn't care. She had to know about Maggie.

They say the truth will set you free, but it was difficult for Jill to believe Maggie was someone Sam knew from his senior year in high school. He really hadn't even talked with this woman—much less seen her at some point? It sounded a little crazy. Sam wouldn't be the first man to lie and try to cover his tracks.

In their six months of dating, Jill had never caught Sam in a lie. He did what he said he was going to do. He always was where he said he was. There were no lies covered up with other lies. No fantastical stories that would lead her to believe Sam was gaming the system or playing her.

Everything was patched up with a little time, a few counseling sessions, and a little forgiveness on both sides.

It wasn't long before Sam bought Jill an engagement ring, hired a wedding planner, and reserved the church. Sam convinced Jill to wait another year before they got married. It would give them time to plan the perfect wedding—and it would give Sam time to grow into the idea of spending his life with Jill.

For months, Sam put the truth in the recesses of his mind. For months, he tried to fall madly in love with Jill. She was smart and witty and had a look that would attract any agent from William Morris. At thirty-two—one year younger than Sam—she was well on her way to becoming a partner in a Manhattan law firm that was dripping with prestige.

Procrastination wasn't a word Sam had in his vocabulary. He was disciplined and on top of his game—a trait he inherited from his mother—but when it came to Jill, he couldn't pull the trigger. He couldn't bring himself to tell her it just wasn't going to work. In the end, he knew no decision was a decision. She had to be told.

It was a Friday night. It had been an overcast and cold day, and Sam knew it was going to be a stormy night. As much as he wanted to slip a note under her door or leave a message on her phone, Sam knew Jill had to be told in person. He owed her that much. She had done nothing wrong except trust the man she planned to marry in one week.

There was no reason to waste any time. As soon as he walked into Jill's apartment, Sam told Jill they needed to talk. Sam had thought about doing it at a neutral site, perhaps a restaurant, but he couldn't chance anything going badly in public. He didn't want Jill to be humiliated in front of a group of strangers.

"Jill, I can't go through with the wedding." Sam would never forget those words.

She just looked at him in disbelief. "Surely, this is a joke," she said.

"I'm so sorry, Jill. I'm calling off the wedding." Sam could see the shock registering on her face.

"I don't know what to say. How could you embarrass me this way?"

"There's really nothing I can say to make this better. I've been fooling myself all along. You don't deserve a husband who isn't 100 percent committed to the marriage."

"Forget that I'm devastated. What about my parents? All the money they spent? The guests? The gifts?"

"You can tell your parents I'll pay for all their expenses."

"What's really going on here, Sam? Is there someone else?"

"Actually, yes, there is someone else."

"Do I know her?"

"No, not technically, but it is the person you read about in my journal. She is happily married, as far as I know."

"So let me get this straight. You love a woman from your past who is married? And this someone is not available? When was the last time you spoke with her?"

"Years ago. A lifetime ago, but she's the one for me. I can't get past how I feel, and that is why it's just not fair to you to go through with this."

"How exactly do you suggest I explain this to everyone?"

"It sounds crazy, I know. It is crazy, but it's how I feel. There's no reason to keep going over and over it, Jill. I'm so sorry."

"Quit saying you're sorry because you aren't sorry. Just leave, Sam. Please leave."

It was the last time he saw Jill. He sent her a check for the wedding expenses, and that was that. Thankfully, his next assignment sent him to Europe, so he didn't have to face Jill, her family, or her friends, but that didn't mean Sam could shake the hurt and shame from what he had done to Jill. *Shame is much worse than guilt*, Sam thought. *It's something you bury inside you, and it's hard to shake. They say time heals everything, but whoever said that didn't experience shame in a profound way.* Sam thought he had done the right thing by Jill, but he knew Jill would never believe it.

Sam hated these long, dark nights when he couldn't sleep. He knew what was coming next. He knew he would continue to replay his past. You would think breaking off his wedding with Jill would be a lesson learned, and in a way, it was. He told himself he would never repeat that mistake again. He was only going to marry under the right circumstance—and the right circumstance was Maggie McWilliams. If he had to die alone, so be it.

Then Sam's life took another turn. His career caught fire, and he was getting the best assignments—high-profile ones that gave him name recognition, which meant women were more interested in him than ever. Instead of putting his life in perspective, his pendulum swung in the opposite direction.

Sam decided to institute what he called the ninety-day rule. He would only date a woman for ninety days. He wouldn't lie to her, he wouldn't lead her on, and he wouldn't make promises he couldn't keep. No sex for ninety days. His agent warned him about getting into a situation that would crater his career, and Sam listened to an extent—about half the time.

It was a life that made men envious. Great job, lots of extracurricular activities on the side. Living the life of a single guy. No attachments. No worries. Sam could go where he wanted, when he wanted, and with whom he wanted.

The ninety-day rule worked well. No way to get attracted or attached to someone in three months. It was like Sam was working in a factory, punching out one widget at a time. For the most part, the women he dated weren't interested in long-term relationships. His short-term flings ran the gamut from models to Wall Street bankers to graduate students. At forty, it was easy for Sam to date women slightly older or much younger. The world of dating was his oyster, and he took full advantage of his newfound celebrity.

There was only one problem: Sam's life was really no life at all. Deep down, Sam knew he was on the fast track to nowhere. His agent also saw it.

Sam was lucky. Malcolm Collins was an agent who cared about his clients more than he cared about money. Most of all, he cared about Sam. He didn't want Sam to burn out and flame out. He knew Sam had a great future, and he didn't want anything to get in the way, especially a lifestyle that took more stamina than running a marathon.

"I know you rarely drink, and I know you don't do drugs, Sam, but you've got to slow down a little bit," Malcolm said. "This isn't an intervention, but I've seen this before in my career. Promising athletes and media professionals go under because they live a life they can't sustain over time."

"That's not me."

"I know, Sam. You think you are invincible, but you aren't. They say forty is the new thirty, but you are going in the opposite direction. Pretty soon forty is going to be the new sixty, if you aren't careful."

"You know my work comes first," Sam said. "I never take shortcuts. I'm always prepared. What do you want from me?"

"As crazy as it may sound, I want you to settle down. Find a nice woman. Get married. Have some kids. Work into your sixties. Your forties are going to be the best years of your life, Sam. You will be at the height of your earning power. You will be growing in wisdom and know what you want from life. You will know what you will put up with and what you won't accept. Take it from me, the next decade will be great—if you approach your life in the right way. I am telling you this as a professional and as a friend."

"You have anyone in mind for me?" Sam asked.

"No one in particular. You meet a lot of women. Surely, you will fall in love with one of them sooner or later."

Sam thought about telling Malcolm about Maggie, but he decided against it. *Explaining being in love with a married woman you haven't seen for more than twenty years just doesn't come across as sane.* "It's not that simple, Malcolm. I'll tell you what. I'll think about what you've said. I really will. I promise."

"I've been around you long enough, Sam, to know that look in your eye. You are just trying to placate me right now. Send me on my way."

"You've been a great agent for me, and there is no doubt you earn your money, but I'm going to be all right, I promise."

Sam knew there was more than a grain of truth to what Malcolm Collins was telling him.

Sam really was going to think about what Malcolm said, but deep down, Sam knew he wasn't ready just yet to give up his jet-setting, live-for-the-moment lifestyle. It would be another two years before Sam would embrace a new pattern of living. He would never forget the Saturday night he came home dead tired from working long hours. He couldn't do it any longer. He couldn't keep going. His life was all a façade: shiny and bright on the outside, empty and lonely on the inside. He called his date and canceled. It was time to regroup and find a new path.

Eighteen years later, Sam had found his new path. As he lay in the dark, he said a little prayer. Sam was tired and alone, but for the first time in a long time, he was not lonely.

He knew his fate was in the hands of twentysomething twins named Lucy and Lily. It had to go well at Maggie's. Sam looked at his phone. It was only a few hours before he would be waiting in front of Maggie's house to hear his fate.

Chapter 6

"W hat the—"

"Don't say it, Katherine." Maggie loved her best friend, Katherine McClellan, but she never could get used to Katherine's colorful language.

Maggie and Katherine had been friends for more than twenty years. Katherine worked in the administration building at Northwestern State University and was the point person for every new professor signing up for benefits. There was an immediate attraction. Maggie liked Katherine's sassy nature, and Katherine liked Maggie's down-to-earth sensibility. After David's tragic death, Maggie needed Katherine more than ever.

"I'm in shock," Katherine said. "You met a man. Now that's front-page news. You better start from the beginning. I want to hear every juicy detail. Better yet, I'm coming over right now so we can have a talk."

"It's late," Maggie said. "Can't we do this over the phone?"

"No, ma'am. I'll be there in a few minutes." Katherine thought it would be a long time before Maggie could be with another man—if ever. That's why it was such a shock to hear Maggie say she needed some advice—relationship advice. For all those twenty years of friendship with Maggie, Katherine was sure they had cussed and discussed just about every subject under the sun. For some reason, Katherine knew that the conversation they were about to have was going to be the most important of all.

"I've already poured you a glass of chardonnay," Maggie said, hugging her confidante and leading her by the hand to the living room. Maggie was already wrapped in her terry cloth bathrobe with her initials monogrammed in blue script. Underneath, Maggie wore her favorite baby blue nightgown. Katherine was in her signature green sweatshirt, gray sweatpants, and gray New Balance tennis shoes.

"I've got a feeling you should dump the chardonnay and get me a tall glass of tequila," Katherine said with a grin.

Maggie always had wanted to be Katherine McClellan. They shared a Scottish heritage, but that was about all. Katherine was six feet tall, if she was an inch. Her salt-and-pepper hair was the epitome of elegance. Her almost translucent skin set off her bright red lips. Katherine's gray eyes were as unusual as an earthquake in Louisiana.

"Better to stick with a glass of wine," Maggie said in her best motherly tone. "You have to drive home tonight."

"I can't stay here with you tonight?" Katherine was kidding, but she wanted to see Maggie's reaction.

"No way, no how."

"In that case, you better spill every last detail of this mystery man." Katherine couldn't wait for Maggie to confess. "And I mean every last detail, right down to the color of the buttons on his shirt."

Katherine and Maggie had been through everything together over all these years. Maggie laughed at her friend's corny jokes, cried during movies, and watched their children become adults. Katherine was by Maggie's side within hours of learning David took his life. Katherine never wavered when the horrible news about David hit the newspapers and television.

"Maggie, you know how much you mean to me and how much our friendship means to me. There's not much we wouldn't do for each other."

"That's why I called you tonight, Katherine. More than ever, more than any time in my life, I need you to tell me the truth. Promise?"

"I promise."

"Pinkie swear?"

"Pinkie swear," Katherine said, taking Maggie's hand in hers.

"I'm going to start from the beginning, so be patient with me. This is hard for me, and you may think I'm crazy, because I really might be crazy, but I need for you to look me in the eye and give me an honest assessment. Things are moving so fast my head is swimming, and I'm afraid I can't make rational decisions right now."

"I'm losing my patience already, sister. You better tell me what's going on with you."

"On Friday night, the most amazing or unusual thing happened to me, depending on how you look at it. This man rings my doorbell and then faints as soon as I open the door."

"I would say this guy isn't off to a good start," Katherine said.

"As it turns out, it's someone from my high school days. I haven't seen him since the summer before we left for college. Not once."

"It was nice of him to look you up."

"This is way more than just looking me up. He tells me that he's thought about me ever since high school. He did hear about David, but he didn't know the details until I told him tonight, but here is the big news—he tells me more or less that he loves me and wants to marry me."

"He loves you more or less?"

"More *than* less. He stayed for dinner Friday night. We talked about old times, what he is doing now and what I've been doing. I told him about Lily and Lucy. You know, the usual banter among old friends."

"At some point in your conversation, it sounds like the banter became much more than banter. Don't tell me this guy is married."

"Not only is he single, but he tells me he has never been married. Never. Well, he almost got married once years ago, but he called it off."

"What happened?"

"Katherine, he told me he called it off because he was in love with me, and if he couldn't be married to me, he didn't ever want to be married."

"So this guy is your age and has never been married?"

"Right."

"This is either very romantic—or this guy is a serious stalker candidate."

Maggie said, "That is exactly what I was thinking at the time."

"Does this guy have a name?"

"Sam Roberts."

"So what happens after dinner?"

"Well, it was late—so I invited him to stay here for the night."

"Are you crazy? You don't know if this guy is on the level, or if he is going to cut you into a thousand pieces, and you let him stay the night?"

"It gets worse."

"He drank too much and tried something!"

"No, that's the trouble. He was a perfect gentleman. I was the one who tried something."

"That's not the Maggie Anne I know and love."

"I was so lonely, Katherine. It had been so long since a man held me. I just crawled into bed next to him."

"Is he a good lover?"

"This is how crazy it gets. He didn't try a thing. He just held me all night."

"This guy must love you. Wait a minute. Did you say his name is Sam Roberts?"

"Don't you start, Katherine."

"The same Sam Roberts who was on national television. The sports guy?"

"The same Sam Roberts. I'm so tired of everyone fawning over him."

"Oh my God, he's famous. So let me get this straight.

The famous Sam Roberts from your high school has been in love with you for forty years, and he wants to marry you?"

"That's about the size of it."

"And what did you say?"

"The next morning, I kicked him out of my house. I sent him packing without a cup of coffee or a piece of toast."

"Now, who is the crazy one?"

"He's staying at the Queen Anne House, so I went over there and asked if he could give me a little more time. He took me to dinner at the Landing tonight."

"And how did that go?"

"Really well. We pretended it was our first date. When he got back to my house, I asked him to come in, and I told him the whole sordid story about David. I knew he deserved the truth."

"I know that was hard for you." Katherine gave Maggie a hug.

"I also told him I didn't think it was going to work out because I have a hard time trusting any man after what David did. How could I possibly trust another man?"

"Trust is something you build over time, Maggie. My rule has always been to trust someone until that person proves he or she can't be trusted. That's the only way we can go through life and not go insane."

"Intellectually, I know that, Katherine. I know you are

right. It's just getting my mind around the idea of starting all over again."

"If this is the same guy I remember watching on television, he is easy on the eyes." Katherine had always been a sucker for handsome men.

"Yes, he is handsome." *Handsome,* Maggie thought, *if you like tall men with a great build and a smile that can light up New Orleans.* And Sam was a classy, as well as classic dresser. He liked polos, and he liked solid colors. No plaids or stripes. Maggie could tell Cole Haan was his shoe of choice. Maybe Sam could have bought five thousand-dollar suits, but he preferred to be understated with his ubiquitous blue blazer and khaki slacks.

Sam was age appropriate all right, but he had those boyish good looks that served him so well on television. He looked much younger than his age, which made Maggie wonder if the wear and tear of the past two years made her look older than her years. If Sam really loved her, maybe those tiny crow's feet around her eyes didn't matter much to him. One thing was for sure—Maggie had no interest in plastic surgery.

"If this guy loved you in high school, why didn't you keep seeing him in college?"

"My dad didn't think Sam would amount to much. He wanted me to marry a doctor or lawyer. Sam was an athlete at the time. I thought—or my dad thought—he would be a coach someday and not make very much money. You knew my dad before he and mom died. He was all about money and security. He wanted the same for his only daughter, his only child."

"I want to meet this man. You have to introduce me. Unless, of course, you told him to get lost again."

"You will meet him tomorrow at church."

"He goes to church, too?"

"I'm glad you are sitting down, Katherine. Not only does he go to church—he was a missionary in South America for three years."

"This guy is perfect." Katherine shook her head.

"That's another problem, and I told him so. He seems perfect."

"No person is perfect. We all have our faults. Some of us more than others, and Maggie, I'm an expert when it comes to sin. No person is as good as we think, and no person is as bad as we think. I know how he feels about you, but how do you feel about him? Deep down?"

"That's the other thing I want to tell you, Katherine. Something I've never told anyone, even you. It's about David and me and our marriage."

"You feel guilty because you wanted David to die after the awful thing he did with that teenage girl."

Maggie took a deep breath and exhaled. "Even worse. I killed my husband."

"You did not. David took his own life."

"Not literally. I didn't put the rope around his neck and kick the chair out from under him, but I might as well have."

"Now you are talking crazy, Maggie."

"After all those years of marriage, we settled into a comfortable rhythm. For years, I took David for granted. My life revolved around the twins. I took them to dance classes and to every soccer match. They became my life."

"Do you really think you are the only mother in the whole entire world to devote a great deal of time to her children? Look how they turned out."

"Yes, they are wonderful adults, and I'm so proud of them."

"I don't understand."

"It goes much, much deeper, Katherine. The last few years, we seldom were intimate."

"Do you really think you are the only person married for more than twenty years who would rather get a good night's sleep than—"

"Don't say that word, Katherine. I'm going to break you of that habit if it's the last thing I do."

"Rather than have sex then."

"It goes even deeper."

"Don't keep me guessing."

"I never got over my first love."

"Sam Roberts?"

"Deep down in the recesses of my heart, I knew I loved Sam, but I never wanted to admit it. When he fainted, and I was looking down on him, I knew. I had to be honest. I've never really gotten past my love for Sam."

"How long did you date in high school?"

"Only a few months."

"Maybe I do need a shot of tequila."

"No, I'm almost finished. You have to go home soon."

"This doesn't sound rational."

"Exactly, Katherine. That's what I've been trying to tell you since you came over. This isn't rational, but it's real. Sam is real. He's at the Queen Anne House right now—getting a good night's sleep—and he will be back here in the morning."

"If your head is spinning, Maggie, I bet his is, too."

"So, you see, I neglected David. I drove him to do this horrible thing. I drove him to do something that disgraced his life. We will never remember David the same ever again, don't you see?"

"I see, but you didn't make David have sex with that child. He took his own life. You can't keep blaming yourself,

Maggie. It's not healthy. We've had this talk more than once."

"I'm better now than I was two years ago, but Sam brought these memories back. He didn't mean to, but he did. I've just got to get this back in perspective, think straight, and figure out what I want to do from here." Tears were swelling in the corners of Maggie's eyes.

"How much of this did you tell Sam?"

"Nothing, except the part about David."

"If you want my advice, keep it that way. What's next with Sam?"

"You know I call the girls every Sunday. Sam's going to come over. I'll introduce him to them and see their reaction—and I'll just go from there."

"Sounds like a plan." Katherine gave Maggie another hug.

"He says it is me or no one. Sam said he's not going to marry anyone if he can't marry me. Can you believe it?"

"You may not understand this yet, but it may turn out that my very best friend is the luckiest woman in the world. Besides, if you don't want him, I'll be glad to take him off your hands. Although, I know you are the only one with a chance."

"You better behave tomorrow when you meet Sam. Now, get out of here, young lady. I've got to get some rest. Another big day tomorrow." Maggie managed a smile as she wiped away one more tear from her cheek.

Part III

Sunday Morning

Part III

Sunday
Morning

Chapter 7

S am Roberts couldn't help but laugh out loud. Big man on campus. Acclaimed sports journalist. International celebrity. He didn't feel like such a big deal sitting in his rental car in front of Maggie's house. He didn't know if the tiny beads of sweat played at his temples because it was already eighty degrees at nine o'clock on another August day that would surely climb into the high nineties or if he was worried about what was happening inside the old Victorian in front of him.

It wasn't the first time Sam had sat in a rental car outside Maggie's home. It had been ten years since Sam was this close to Maggie. He had no good reason for impulsively changing his flight from New York to Los Angeles to include a stopover in Louisiana. Sam grabbed a commuter flight from Dallas to Shreveport, and then he headed seventy-eight miles straight south to Natchitoches. That hour-long drive was less than scenic and gave Sam plenty of time to reflect on just why he had detoured.

The thought of seeing and talking with Maggie was overwhelming. He had to do it—even if it were only for a few minutes. It really didn't matter to Sam if Maggie's husband was around or not. Sam parked a stone's throw from Maggie's front door and sat frozen in the front seat, rehearsing what he would say to Maggie. In the end, it didn't matter; he never had the courage to ring the doorbell. After two hours, Sam cranked his Chevrolet Impala and headed for the Shreveport airport on his way to California.

How many nights in the Amazon had Sam crawled under his mosquito netting, stared at the ceiling, and prayed to God that someday Maggie would be his wife? He was ashamed because mixed with his prayer was a wish that Maggie and David would get a divorce. Sometimes, Sam would fantasize that David would die. Nothing horrible. Perhaps a stroke in his sleep. Just quick and painless. Now, Sam felt even more guilty because David had done just that—died—and it was a horrible death. His death took his life and fractured a family.

Sam remembered the day he heard that David had died. The obituary said it was a "short illness." Short illness was the code phrase for suicide. Not always, but sometimes. Sam felt badly for Maggie and her family. He didn't want to be a home-wrecker, and he wasn't. Not that he could have wrecked her home. He decided long ago to keep up with Maggie from a distance, bide his time, and let life play out.

It took two years for the news to reach Sam in Brazil, and he was glad. As much as he would have liked to console Maggie at the time of her husband's death, he knew she needed time. Time to heal, time to make sure her kids were all right. Sam had waited long enough—three-fourths of his life.

Now Maggie was in control. All Sam could do was wait to see if Maggie invited him in or send him on his way.

Since Lily and Lucy had joined the Peace Corps in Thailand, it had become a custom for Maggie and the girls to FaceTime every Sunday morning. It seemed a little crazy because nine o'clock in the morning in the United States meant it was nine o'clock at night in Thailand. The twins were young; they could handle it. Maggie was pretty sure they were up all hours of the night anyway. Her girls didn't sleep a lot when they were in high school and college, so why would the Peace Corps be any different?

"Anything new this week?" Maggie's opening line was almost always the same.

"Teaching English is so rewarding that we could tell

you a new story every five minutes, Mom." Lucy was exaggerating a bit, but she knew her mother, the professor, loved to hear their stories.

"We have one youngster who brings us a flower every week," Lily added. "All the kids and their parents are so appreciative of what we are doing."

"And the classes?"

"About 99 percent of our students desperately want to learn English, and they work extra hard to speak the language," Lucy said. "They even teach us a bit of Thai along the way."

"Are you seeing a little more of the country?" It was a trick question.

"Not too much," Lily said. "We stick close to home because we work so much. Eventually, we will get to travel more."

"I hope you are careful. I worry about you so much. I know you rave about the Thai people, and I don't doubt you are telling the truth, but please, for my sake, be careful. I couldn't bear it if something happened to either one of you."

"We aren't CIA operatives, Mom," Lily said. "Everything is fine. You taught us well. We are adults now, remember?"

Maggie knew her twins were well into adulthood, but they would always be twelve years old in her mind. They would always be her little girls. That's just the way it is with all parents. No matter how smart, no matter how mature, no matter how knowledgeable about the ways of the world, it is a mother's duty to worry about her children. It's been that way since the beginning of time.

"Fine, I'll stop my usual Sunday morning interrogation," Maggie said. "I miss you both."

"So how are you, Mom?" Lily asked.

"Well, now that you've asked, I've got some big news for you."

"Do tell," Lucy said.

"I would like for you to meet someone," Maggie said.

"It might be a year before that could happen, Mom," Lucy said.

"Actually, he is outside right now. I could bring him in and let you meet him."

"Outside?" the twins almost shouted together.

"I told him to wait in the car until I gave him the okay. I wanted your permission to bring him in to say hello."

"This is not like you, Mom. You need to be honest with us."

"This is a man I've known most of my life. We dated for a little while in high school, and then we went our separate ways. He knocked on my door on Friday afternoon, and he's been here with me for the past couple days. I don't mean *with* me; he decided to stay in Natchitoches for the weekend."

"If you have him outside of our house, it sounds like you want us to meet him," Lily said.

"What do you think, Lucy?"

"Mom, if you want us to meet him, then bring him inside. Who is this mystery man?"

"Before I tell you his name, I want to give you a little background. It's going to sound a little crazy, but just hang in with me while I explain."

"We will try," Lily said.

"But no promises," Lucy added.

"He says he loves me and wants to marry me."

"Wow, are you kidding me?" Lily said.

"I'm not kidding. It gets even crazier. He's never been married because he said he only wanted to marry me."

"And he's your age, right?" Lucy said.

"I am seven days older than he is, but that's beside the point. I loved him—or I thought I loved him—when we dated, but my father insisted that I break up with him when I left for college. We drifted apart, and I ended up marrying your father."

"And you haven't talked with him all these years?" Lucy asked.

"Never. He and I have never talked. I sort of vaguely heard

about him from time to time, but we never communicated until Friday afternoon."

"How do you feel about him, Mom?" Lily asked.

"Okay, ready? I said it's getting crazy, so here is the craziest thing—I'm glad he is here."

"What does that mean?" Lucy asked.

"It means I think I like him a lot."

"What does that mean?" Lily asked.

"It means just what it means. I like him very much. We've had a great time for the past day and a half."

"Do you love this guy?" Lucy asked.

"Maybe."

Lucy said, "Maybe, yes, you do love him, but you don't want us to freak out, or maybe you don't know for sure because of what you went through with Dad?"

"Maybe, yes, I do love him, and I don't want you girls to freak out."

"Wow!" Lucy said.

"You better bring him in; we've got to meet this guy. You agree, Lily?"

Lily nodded her head up and down.

"Fine. I'll ask him to come meet you."

"Are you going to tell us his name, for heaven's sake?" Lily asked.

"No. I'll introduce you in a minute. I'll be right back."

On her way outside, Maggie thought she was having an out-of-body experience. Did she really just tell her daughters that she might be in love with someone she hadn't seen in four decades? Someone she'd only seen for a few hours? What in the world was she thinking?

Sam was sitting behind the wheel of his red rental with the windows rolled down.

Maggie felt a tiny bit guilty that she had made him wait outside this whole time, but she didn't know how Lucy and Lily would react. She motioned for him to come inside. "Lily and Lucy would like to meet you, Sam. Do you still want to come say hello?"

"If I can wait here for thirty minutes with sweat dripping into my eyes, you know that I'm serious about meeting your daughters. Can I have a minute to freshen up before the introductions?"

"No problem. Just come into the study when you are ready."

Maggie went back to her laptop and said, "He will be here in a minute. He wanted to freshen up a bit."

Sam was true to his word. He didn't want to keep the twins waiting too long. He put some water on his face, made sure his hair was presentable, and found his way to the study. From his professional life, he knew the importance of first impressions.

"Lily and Lucy, I would like for you to meet Sam Roberts. Sam, this is Lily and Lucy."

"You really are identical twins." Sam immediately knew he had said the wrong thing. "I apologize. I know you hear that kind of thing all the time."

"Lucy is on the left," Maggie said.

"Sam Roberts? That sounds familiar," Lily said. "Oh, my God. Oh, my God. Are you serious, Mom? *The* Sam Roberts?"

"Yes, Lily. *The* Sam Roberts," Maggie said.

"Somehow this guy isn't registering with me," Lucy said.

"Lucy, Sam Roberts. Remember when we were playing soccer, and we would watch the World Cup to get some pointers? Sam Roberts was the play-by-play announcer for all World Cup soccer events. Am I wrong, Mr. Roberts?"

"It's Sam—and you aren't wrong. You have a good memory like your mother."

"Mom, you are telling Lucy and me that the man who has loved you his whole entire life and has never married because he's only loved you his whole entire life is *the* Sam Roberts?"

"I guess that's what I'm telling you."

"I see your mother has filled both of you in on what's been going on the past couple of days."

"*The* Sam Roberts," Lucy said. "Mom, could you give us just a minute with Mr. Roberts—Sam—alone?"

"Whatever you have to say, you can't say it in front of me?" Maggie didn't want to leave Sam alone with the twins. She didn't know exactly where the conservation was heading.

"Please, Mom. Trust us," Lucy said.

"It's okay, Maggie. I'm a big boy. I'll be all right."

Now it was Maggie's turn to be on the outside looking in. If the girls wanted some privacy with Sam, she would honor their request. She decided to go to her bedroom to avoid the temptation to listen in on their conversation.

"Sam, as you might imagine, Lily and I are a little taken aback. It's a lot to process in such a short period of time."

"I can only imagine what you might be thinking," Sam said.

"Well, let me tell you exactly what I'm thinking. I remember reading about you in *People* magazine. You were one of the most eligible bachelors in America. You also went through about a million women … if the rumors were correct."

"I see where you are going with this, Lucy," Lily said. "Our mother is vulnerable and probably still a little raw from what my dad did to all of us. The last thing she needs is to be hurt."

"I know exactly what you are saying," Sam said. "You have no way of knowing this, but I have no intention of hurting your mother. I only want to love her. I *do* love her."

"You must admit, this is very, very bizarre," Lucy said. "I don't know what to say. My mom's dad is no longer with us, so I'll ask the same question he would have asked: What is your intent with our mom?"

"I want to marry her and spend our remaining years together. I want to make her happy every day we are married because being with her will make me happy every day of my life."

"You are smooth, Mr. Roberts. I will give you that much. I guess what I'm saying is that if you hurt my mother in any way, Lily and I will hunt you to the ends of the earth. I don't mean to sound dramatic, but that is a promise. We love our mother very much, and she has had a huge cross to bear. She can't bear another one."

"Understood. If I leave without marrying your mother, it will be because it was her decision—not mine. If she wants me to leave, I'll leave. If she wants me to be in her life, I'll be thrilled."

"Lily and I are out of the house now, so this is all about Mom. If Mom wants you with her, then we will accept her decision. We trust our mom to make good choices. She always has. Even with our dad. He was a good husband and a good dad until something went haywire in his brain. Lily and I just want to remember the good things."

"If things work out, I'm looking forward to getting to know both of you. In my heart and in my head, I can see the future, and the future is bright, but it's not just up to me. Your mom has to say yes."

"Fair enough," Lucy said. "Just so you know where we stand. Please ask our mother to come back in now … if you don't mind."

Maggie had a little taste of what it must have been like for Sam to wait in his car that morning. It was only a few minutes, but it seemed like an hour and a half.

"What do you think, girls?" Maggie knew the twins were a good judge of character.

"We are with you, Mom, in whatever you decide," Lucy said. "We love you and only want the best for you."

"We love you, Mom," Lily said.

"Sam, could you give us one more minute with our mother?" Lucy asked.

"Sure. It was nice meeting both of you. I've heard so many good things already, and I'm looking forward to getting to know both of you."

"I'll be right there, Sam," Maggie said. "If you wait by the front door, I'll be ready to go to church in a minute."

Sam didn't know exactly what to think, but he had to

take Lucy and Lily at their word. They really did want the best for their mom—and that was all he could ask for because that's what he wanted, too.

"Mom, this is so fast for us, but you know your heart. I still can't get over the fact that this larger-than-life person has carried a torch for you ever since high school. That is amazing. If he is telling the truth, the next chapter in your life will be incredible."

"I haven't decided anything yet, but you two will be the first to know. And, don't worry, you always will be number one in my life."

"We know, Mom," Lily said.

"Sam Roberts," Lucy repeated. "I just can't get over it. Someday, my mom could be Mrs. Sam Roberts."

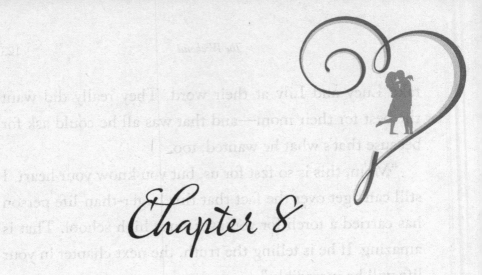

Chapter 8

S'am had seen his share of churches, but the basilica in Natchitoches was among the most beautiful. Like the city itself, the basilica dated back to the 1700s. The church had gone through several incarnations, but it was classic in every sense of the word. Parishioners, or anyone visiting the basilica, would use words like *majestic* or *regal*. With its sky-high ceiling, beautiful stained glass, and classic sanctuary, the Basilica of the Immaculate Conception was truly worthy of being on the National Register of Historic Places. Sam was a little envious of Maggie. This was her parish, her church family. Perhaps, God willing, it would be his church, as well.

Sunday morning Mass was as traditional as the church, with one exception. The message from the priest was as modern and fresh as the church was old. It was centered on what we should be doing in our world—bringing the message of good news to everyone we meet, with nonjudgmental dignity and respect. Sam could get used to coming here every Sunday.

Maggie was taking a chance in bringing Sam to Mass. After all, they were her friends, people she had known most of her adult life, and she was hoping they would trust her as much as her own children did. Maggie knew Katherine would be first to greet to Sam after the service.

"Where have you been keeping this gorgeous man?" Katherine asked with her biggest smile.

"Sam, meet my best friend, Katherine. Katherine, this is Sam. Now, behave yourself, Katherine."

"Katherine, any friend of Maggie's is a friend of mine," Sam said, shaking her hand.

"Don't worry, Sam. If you hang around Maggie, you will be seeing a lot of me."

"Sounds good to me," Sam said.

"Katherine, we would like to stay and talk, but Sam and I have to go across the street to get coffee and talk. Call me later?"

"If you insist. Sure I can't tag along?"

"More than sure, Katherine."

"I'll get all the dirt later anyway."

"Bye, Katherine."

"Goodbye, Sam. I hope to see you again soon."

Maggie waved hello to a few more friends and then headed across the street to the Merci Beaucoup. She and Sam found a corner table, ordered two cups of coffee and two beignets and settled in for what Sam expected to be a long chat. No problem for him; he liked their talks.

"What did you think of the girls?"

"You should be so proud, Maggie. They are smart and confident, and they love their mother."

"What did they ask you when I left the room?"

"They just wanted to be sure I was for real—that's all. You can't blame them."

"This is all moving so fast for me, Sam. I can only imagine what they are thinking."

"They are thinking they don't want to see their mother get hurt."

"*I* don't want to see their mother get hurt," Maggie said.

That brought a big smile to Sam's face. "It's the last thing I want, too."

"I have a couple of more things I want to get straight," Maggie said. "When David was alive, we would serve as mentors for engaged couples. That's pretty ironic now, isn't it? Well, part of that process is rating the compatibility of the couple to prepare them better for marriage."

"You want to know if we are compatible?"

"Frankly, yes. What are the big things that stand in

the way of making a marriage work?" Maggie was in her teacher mode.

"Well, I suspect money, sex, faith, stuff like that," Sam said.

"Exactly, and that's what I want to talk about for a few minutes."

"I'm ready. I have faith, I like money, and I like sex."

"Be serious, Sam. Can we talk about these things? They are on my mind."

"I'm sorry. Sure."

"We might as well start with money. You have been a missionary the last few years, and I know that doesn't pay much."

"One hundred and fifty dollars a month," Sam offered.

"I know you worked, but you don't have an income. Am I wrong? You can imagine what a professor makes."

"I don't have an income, that's right, but I've saved my pennies over the years, and I'm doing okay. Besides, if I have to go back to work, I can always get a job."

"I know, but not here in Natchitoches. There aren't many jobs for sports journalists in this area. In fact, there aren't any such jobs anywhere close to Natchitoches. One thing I do know is I don't want to move. I love it here. My friends are here, my church is here, and my work is here."

"We can live here if that is what you want. The more I

see of the city, the more I like it. I'm willing to live wherever you want, Maggie, as long as I'm with you."

"I don't have a desire to support you in my old age. No offense," Maggie said.

"No offense taken. I just think we can work through this money thing. I may be wrong, but I think I have enough saved to take care of things. If not, I'll find a job right here in Natchitoches."

"In that case, we might as well get right down to the sex thing," Maggie said. "You've barely kissed me, much less tried to have sex with me. Do you like sex?"

"Do *you* like sex?"

"I asked first."

"Maggie, I like sex as much as the next person. Remember, I told you I was almost married at one time. I've been here and there over the years. Now, you can answer me."

"David and I had what I would consider a normal sex life. Like most couples, more in the beginning of our marriage, less intimacy the last few years. I enjoyed our time together."

"So you've had sex with one person your entire life? Is that right?"

"I've never thought of it quite like that, Sam, but, yes, I never had an affair, if that is what you are asking."

"That's not what I'm asking. I would never ask that, but here is what I'm saying. I'm not worried about having sex with you. I don't feel like we are under any pressure to perform."

"I know we aren't kids, but I think it's important that we are compatible in bed."

"I have no doubt we will be sensational," Sam said. "For me, it's all about love. I love you. You love me. You are right. We aren't over the hill, but we are, let's say, in our mature years. When it comes to good sex, we can figure this out. I just have to know what makes you happy. That's it. I know I'll be happy. I really don't see a problem."

"It's a concern. That's all, Sam."

"I'll tell you what. We can go back to your house right now and make love. Or, if you really want to spice it up, we can go to the Queen Anne House and pretend we are on our honeymoon. I just think it would be better—perfect, in fact—if we waited until we were married. In my mind, that will be soon."

"Do you have an answer for everything, Sam?"

"When you were mentoring young couples, did you tell them to have sex early and often—or did you tell them to wait?"

"Trust me, Sam, they didn't wait. In fact, a majority live together before they get married, but we did counsel them to have a waiting period before the wedding ceremony so the honeymoon would be a special time."

"That exactly describes our situation. We didn't wait either. We've had sex, just not with each other. I think you are very sexy, and I am hoping you think I'm a little bit sexy. I'm 100 percent confident we are going to be like a couple of twentysomethings when the time comes."

"You do have an answer for everything."

"It's hard to believe I'm trying to talk you out of having sex, but it can be very special if we wait for the honeymoon. But, if you absolutely insist, I'm ready to go."

"It's probably less complicated if we wait," Maggie said.

"Exactly. I'll tell you what, Maggie." Sam sipped his coffee. "Stand up."

"What are you up to now, Sam Roberts?"

"Just stand up, and I'll show you."

Maggie slid her chair back and stood while Sam did the same. Sam took Maggie into his arms, squeezed tight, and gave her a long kiss. The patrons at the other tables began to clap.

"I'm against most public displays of affection," Sam said, sitting back down, "but this just seemed like the right thing to do."

"I must say, it felt extraordinary," she said, still flush from the experience. "You are a good kisser, for sure."

"See? That's what I've been trying to tell you all along. We are going to be great together."

"Two more things, Sam."

"Shoot."

"We do have our faith in common. My church means a lot to me. I think you could tell that this morning. I know your faith means a lot to you; otherwise, you wouldn't have been a missionary for three years. However, I do feel guilty about your missionary work."

"Guilty? How?"

"I feel like I'm taking you away from where God wants you to be—in Brazil. If you need to be serving in Brazil, I'll understand."

"As I mentioned, my contract is up. I've served my three years. Make no mistake, I've loved every minute of it, but it's time for my life to take another turn—with you or without you."

"So, if you weren't with me, you would go back to Brazil?"

"Maybe, but probably not. I'm too old to live in those conditions for much longer. I'm in good shape, but living in a third world kind of environment takes its toll. Honestly, they probably wouldn't let me go back."

"So have you thought about what you would do?"

"Write a book, get a doctorate degree, serve with a nonprofit wherever I live. I don't know. Right off the top of my head, that's what I'm thinking. That's my best guess."

"Are you sure you would be happy in Natchitoches? It's not for everyone, especially someone like you."

"What does that mean?"

"You've lived in New York, and you've traveled the world. This is a quiet, quaint little village. It's wonderful for me, but you might get bored."

"You've already told me that this is where you will live out your life, right? If I'm with you, I can live anywhere. Let me ask you something. Do you like to travel?"

"Yes, but I've only been to a few places."

"If we live here, we can travel, experience other cultures, see other cities, and explore other countries."

"Sure. I would love to travel."

"Travel is only a function of two things: time and money."

"I guess that brings us back to money, Sam."

"If we can afford to go, we'll go. If not, we'll stay at home and grow old together."

"One more thing before we go."

"I'm ready."

"Lily and Lucy. They are everything to me, Sam. We were close before David's stupidity, but we've become even closer since the tragedy. Where do you think you fit with us?"

"I would never, ever attempt to come between you and your children. Besides, I know the answer if I forced you to make a choice between me and Lucy and Lily. I would be in third place. So it would be crazy for me to make any demands when it comes to your children."

"In this case, that is the right answer. No one and nothing will ever come between me and my girls."

"Nor should it. You have a family history, and I know very little about it—but I'm willing to learn, to invest myself, and to immerse myself into your life. I look forward to getting to know Lily and Lucy, and hopefully, they will come to accept me over time. They will accept me because they will see that I've made you happy. They will see that I'm not going anywhere. They will see that I respect their place with you. I've got this whole thing planned out, Maggie."

"It sounds like you've thought about this a lot."

"Only for about forty years or so. That's a lot of time for a man to determine what he wants in life, what makes him happy. Being married to you would make me happy, Maggie."

"I guess I've got some thinking to do then."

"How about this? I'm starving to death. Why don't we go back to your house, change clothes, go to the store for fruit, crackers, and cheese, and have a picnic?"

"You know it's going to be ninety-six degrees this afternoon."

"So we'll find a shade tree. There's a little breeze. We can do this."

"Why not? It's been forever since I've been on a picnic. That sounds wonderful."

"We've had enough serious talk—so let's go have some fun."

"Great. That's a plan."

"And no sex." Sam couldn't help himself.

Chapter 9

For Maggie, there was something special about the lake. When she brought the kids to Cane River Lake all those years ago, it was so peaceful, so calm. The lake, not the twins. She would sit on a quilt and watch the shimmering water, rays of sun skimming along the surface. The children were happy swimming in the clear, blue water and playing hide-and-seek in the forest.

Maggie believed there was something magical about bodies of water. It could be a lake, a river, or the ocean. It didn't matter. When you were there, you could feel a very real energy flowing through your body. Maggie especially loved the ocean, but that wasn't possible living in Natchitoches. She had to settle for the lake, which wasn't a bad alternative. Lucy and Lily loved the lake, and, if the kids were happiest at the lake, then Maggie was happiest at the lake. She always thought it was the kids' happiness that made her happy, but now that she was at the water's edge once again, Maggie knew differently.

There was a reason Maggie had a warm feeling inside, and she had to come to grips with it. Cane River Lake reminded Maggie of that summer after high school when she and Sam would go to the lake and sit for hours to talk. They could solve most of the problems of the world in just a few hours.

"This always has been a special place for me, Sam. The water, Lucy and Lily having such a grand time. David never came with us. He always was too busy with work, but I didn't mind. I was content just to be with the kids and the water."

"I know how much you like the ocean," Sam said, spreading the quilt on the ground. "The waves, the smell. When I was in Brazil, I would close my eyes and imagine the ocean. Every time I was in some kind of a funk, I would focus on the power of the ocean and somehow feel a little better."

"I feel drawn to the water's siren song, but there's something more for me. I didn't understand it until we came here today. I still have those memories of us, and those memories make me happy. For a brief moment that summer after high school, you made me feel so special, so alive, so important, like I was the only woman on earth. I haven't really felt that way since."

"You know, that was a special time for me, too. It was the summer I fell in love. There is nothing like your first love. You want to cry, laugh, and shout from the top of your lungs, 'I am in love.' You don't care who thinks you are crazy because you know how you feel. The first love is forever imprinted in your heart."

"I was so dumb and naive, Sam. I'm so sorry."

"No, don't ever say that. You were young. I was young. Who knew that I really loved you for sure, for real? Everybody thought we were just kids with a crush. Everyone has a first love, but not everyone makes it their last love. You were a normal—never average—young woman who was ready to experience life. That's all. There's no reason to apologize."

Maggie was grateful Sam had suggested a picnic at the lake. It was a beautiful afternoon—a few fluffy clouds to hide the sun just enough to keep the temperature at a reasonable level—and the humidity, which was usually off the charts at that time of year, wasn't too bad.

As they sat on the quilt, Sam noticed it was the same quilt they used all those years ago. Maggie had inherited the quilt from her mother, a treasure handed down from generation to generation, and it was now only used for special occasions.

Maggie's mother always said, "Everything happens for a reason." Maggie had to admit she sometimes couldn't find a reason for events in her life. Why did she marry David? Why did she become content with an average marriage?

"I admire you, Sam Roberts." Maggie opened the picnic basket and took out two Diet Dr Peppers, crackers, cheese, and apple slices. "You have done so much with your life."

"Don't be too sure. I've had a good life, but I have always wondered if it could have been more. Or, in a strange way, maybe I would have been happier if it had been less."

"You lost me, Sam."

"You know, a quiet life with a wife, two kids, a dog, nine-to-five job, little house with a white picket fence."

"Do you mean that?"

"Oh, I've thought about it a lot. My male friends envied me. The man about town. A new woman every week. Although, that was their fantasy. There was never a woman every week. Going to all those exotic places. Getting paid for what you love to do. Don't get me wrong. I did love my work, but something was missing."

"Brazil?"

"No. You."

Sam took a slow sip of his Diet Dr Pepper, put it on top of the picnic basket, and took Maggie's hand. He brought her hand to his lips and gently kissed it. "I'm glad you let me come into your home on Friday night."

"I didn't think I had much of a choice, since you fainted, but I'm glad you decided to come to my corner of the world this weekend," Maggie said.

"The weekend isn't over yet, but I appreciate the compliment. Would you do me a favor?"

Maggie was a little weary of men asking for favors, but this was Sam. "What is it?"

"Don't move. I'll be right back." Sam was on his feet in record time, heading for the car. He lifted the trunk.

Maggie couldn't tell what he was doing, but she saw a camera in his hand. "No, please don't. I'm a mess today. Can't I have time to fix my hair and makeup a little before you point that thing at me?"

"I promise it won't take long. I'll work fast. Besides, you look beautiful just like that. There is one thing you can count on: I'll never lie to you." Sam hoped is words didn't remind Maggie of her husband. He couldn't imagine any reason to lie to Maggie, especially about her stunning looks. Maggie was striking on this lazy summer afternoon in her pale pink sundress and natural leather sandals. What he loved about her most was her cream-colored floppy straw hat. The tiny holes in the hat reflected on Maggie's face and made her look like she had a million freckles. It reminded

Sam of the stars in the heavens, each one unique, just like the woman he was with on this afternoon.

"I'll do it only if I get to shoot a photo of you," Maggie said, taking off her classic tortoise-shell Ray-Bans.

"Deal. Now, sit back and look up at me."

Because of her dance background, Maggie was just as comfortable in front of the camera as she was in front of an audience. Sam asked Maggie to take off her hat as he adjusted the lens. He was waiting for a cloud to cover the sun so her face would have a soft glow.

For the next few minutes, Maggie felt like a fashion model on location.

Even looking through the lens of his camera, Sam made her feel special. As the camera's motor drive whirled, Maggie would tilt her head at a slight angle, smile, and then close her lips for a more subtle pose.

After fifteen or twenty shots, Maggie was into the pseudo professional photo session, trusting her photographer to take care of all the details. How she wanted a man to help her take care of the details—a man who would be there for her, as the vow says, "for better or worse."

"Hey, it's my turn to take your photo."

"Just one more, I promise."

"That's what every photographer says. One more turns

into a hundred more. Give me that camera right now, Mr. Roberts."

Maggie was playful, but Sam could tell she meant business. Besides, it wasn't a problem because he had captured the image he wanted. He handed over the Canon and sat on the quilt.

"I think I want you closer to the lake, if you don't mind." Maggie looked down at the camera and discovered it was set on manual. "You don't play fair. I don't know how to shoot on a manual setting. You better put it on automatic pilot for me."

"We can shoot my photo another day."

"No way, big boy. This is going to happen. We have a deal."

As they walked toward the water, Sam could tell Maggie had a certain photo in mind.

"Why don't we get someone to take our picture, so we will have one of us by the water? We both love the water so much."

"Tomorrow, I promise. Not today. I hate to keep repeating myself, but trust me."

"I don't know what you have up your sleeve, Sam, but it sounds like a trick to me. Women's intuition."

"You are way too smart for your own good. Do you know that?"

"Okay, I'll photograph you today—and you promise we'll find someone to shoot our photo tomorrow?"

"I promise. Make this as quick and painless as possible. That's my only request."

Maggie positioned Sam with the sun at her back. She was standing on a picnic table, slightly looking down at him, which was the only way she could get a good angle, adjusting her five-foot-eight frame to his six-foot-two body.

She didn't know much about photography, but she understood that shooting a person's photo from the ground up wasn't very flattering. Maggie generally used her phone to take pictures, and the rapid motion of the Canon's motor drive scared her. She flinched and blurred the first photo.

It didn't take long for her to make the adjustment, and she was satisfied with the last two or three images she shot. Since she was used to shooting only one or two photos of each subject anyway, it wasn't a big deal. Sam was a gorgeous man—even in a T-shirt and shorts. "I really would like a photo of us together, Sam."

"Tomorrow, I promise. Come hell or high water—and I don't like hell and I don't like high water—I'll make it happen. I want a photo of us much more than you can ever know."

Sam took the camera from Maggie and headed to the car. He didn't want to get dirt in the lens.

By the time Sam returned, Maggie was putting all the leftover food in her basket. She took two plastic drinking cups and filled them with Diet Dr Pepper.

The afternoon went so fast, Maggie thought. *It is so relaxing out by the lake—and being with Sam makes it even better.*

"Do me one last favor." Sam had a childlike quality to his face, almost like he was caught with his hand in the candy jar. "Lie down on the quilt."

Maggie gave him a quizzical look, but did as he asked.

"Don't worry," Sam said, lying down beside her. "It's going to be all right. Look at those clouds."

For a few minutes, Maggie and Sam stared at the sky, looking at the fluffy white pillows moving slowly, much more like a tortoise than the hare. Neither of them said a word. Both were content in the moment. Neither wanted the afternoon to end.

"They are so beautiful," Maggie said, breaking the silence.

"Tell me what you see," Sam said.

Maggie began to study the clouds more closely. There were so many.

"I see so many things, so many possibilities."

"That's good, but what do you specifically see?"

"I see my children floating by as happy as they can be. And see that little cloud next to those three big clouds?"

Maggie pointed. "That little cloud reminds me of my guardian angel. She looks after me. I don't go anywhere without her. Maybe it was my guardian angel who sent you to me this weekend."

Sam reached over and intertwined his fingers with hers. They continued to stare at the clouds as the sun played hide and seek.

"I love that image. Your guardian angel. Maybe my guardian angel knows your guardian angel. Did you ever think of that possibility? Wouldn't that be convenient. Maybe our guardian angels are meant to be together for all eternity."

"That would mean we would have to stay together," Maggie said. "Maybe we should ask them what we should do."

"Be my guest."

"You are the missionary. I thought you would have the secret code to unlock the main gate up there."

"Sorry to disappoint you, but I'm no better or worse than anyone else. In fact, I'm sure you are a much better person than me."

"I doubt it. I can't tell you how many times I've been mad at God in the past few years. How many times I've almost given up believing in the past few years."

"That's normal. Be mad. God can take it."

"Really? I thought Catholics were supposed to have faith no matter what happens in this life. I was taught God would love us and protect us no matter what comes our way."

"Remember what Mother Teresa once said?"

"Saint Teresa, now."

"See, you are more Catholic than any missionary."

"What did Saint Teresa of Calcutta say?"

"She said God never gives us more than we can handle. I just wish He didn't trust me so much."

"Amen to that."

"But you hung in there better, I suspect, than most people. Now you are coming out the other side."

"Some days are better than others—even after all this time."

"God does love us. I believe that. Faith is hard—I don't care what anyone says. I've always said the problem with church is that there are too many human beings involved."

"Some days, I think I've wasted my entire life, Sam. Some days, I think it's just that I'm going through a midlife crisis. Either way, I could have done so much more with my life. I could have helped so many more people. I could have been there more for my children and my husband. I could go on and on."

"I've got some startling news for you, Maggie. We are *all* imperfect. All of us could have done better. I've done a lot of things that I would be embarrassed for you to know. Hopefully, I've learned a little along the way. Sometimes I make the same dumb mistakes over and over, but I get up the next day and keep trying."

"My dream was to be a ballet dancer on the world stage, and I never even got close,"

"Are you really sorry you didn't pursue your dance career?"

"I don't dwell on it. After all, how many years do you have as a professional dancer? Maybe ten or fifteen years? I probably wasn't that good anyway."

"What was the trade-off?"

"My family."

"From my perspective, that's not a bad trade-off. You have your children for a lifetime. That's a lot longer than ten or fifteen years. Besides, didn't you help out at a dance studio once upon a time?"

"How did you remember that, Sam?"

"Good reporting, but didn't you teach dance?"

"That's right. I loved teaching those youngsters."

"How many children did you help? How many young women have more confidence and good self-esteem because you were in their lives? How many people have confidence because you taught them balance and grace? How many have an appreciation for the arts because you instilled in them the beauty of dance?"

"Where were you when I could have used a marketing director?"

"If I could go back, Maggie, there are things I would change in my life."

"Like what?"

"I would have been more focused on the spiritual side of life rather than my have-a-good-time mentality. I could have helped more people."

"You were so successful in your career. You brought pleasure to millions of people. That is the very definition of success."

"In some way, yes, but does that really count for much?"

"Maybe not as much as what you are doing now, but it counts."

Even though she had started the conversation, Maggie was ready to change the subject. "What do you see in the clouds, Sam?"

Sam decided to take his time because there was no greater pleasure on earth than lying on your back on a warm day and staring at a blue sky sprinkled with puffy, white clouds. He had done it many times in Brazil. Every cloud somehow reminded him of Maggie.

"You."

"No, silly. Really."

"You. I promise. I can't tell you how many times I have done this in the past few years. I would go outside my house, lie on the ground, and watch clouds crawl past me. As much as I tried to visualize puppies or the ocean, they weren't there. Only you."

"What do I look like in a Brazilian sky?"

"At peace with yourself, with life."

"If only that were the truth." Maggie recalled all the days she thought about her marriage and what she could have done better. She remembered all those nights when she couldn't sleep, when she would toss and turn, and lay in her pitch-black bedroom for hours, wiping tears from her eyes. No, she was one hundred and eighty degrees from peaceful.

"Don't forget, all of us have good days and bad days, ups and downs. We may have bad years, but we also have good years. When you really reflect on your life, what do you see?" Sam could see a hint of hesitation in Maggie's eyes. "Quit stalling, young lady."

"Do journalists always ask the right questions? I guess I shouldn't complain. I have my health. The twins are doing well under the circumstances. Other than my life completely falling apart a couple of years ago, I guess the only complaint I have is that life goes by so quickly."

Life goes by so quickly. Sam was excited that he and

Maggie were on the same page. He wanted to instill that sense of urgency in her so he could nudge her into marrying him. Even under the best of circumstances, he and Maggie only had twenty-five years of quality life to share, give or take a couple of years.

He would rather have had fifty or sixty years with Maggie, but that ship sailed a long time ago. He and Maggie were right here, right now, and Sam didn't want to waste another minute, much less another day, week, or month.

"That's why it's so important to celebrate each day, live life to the fullest. Not that I practice what I preach. I've had many lonely days and nights because that was the world I created for myself. I don't know if it is good or bad, but being here feels good."

"I know it sounds selfish, but I'm glad in some strange way that you waited for me all these years. It's almost unbelievable. I certainly don't deserve your affection, and I certainly haven't earned your love."

"Love isn't earned, Maggie. My love isn't predicated on you loving me. The definition of superficial love is 'I'll love you if you love me.' I love you because I love you, whether you love me or not. Of course, it works best when we love each other." Sam remembered a couple he knew years ago who were madly in love after thirty-five years of marriage. He asked the husband once to share the key to such a happy marriage. The husband said it was because he and his wife had learned to compromise early in their marriage.

"For example," the husband said, "my wife likes to go the beach on vacation, and I like to go the mountains. So one year, we go to the beach, and the next year—we go the beach. And, for thirty-five years, we've gone to the beach."

That was the most beautiful definition of unconditional love Sam had ever heard. His friend wanted his wife to be happy—no matter what. Sam also knew the wife went out of her way to sacrifice for her husband.

"I wish I could have said that about my marriage," Maggie said.

"Don't be so hard on yourself. More people should be like you. If I were a betting man, and I'm not, I bet you did the best you could. You were there for your husband and your children. In the end, that's what matters. You were a good wife and a good mother."

"It's taken me a long time to come to grips with my life. I'm feeling better every day about where I've been, and I'm looking forward to where I'm going. It's just so hard sometimes."

"Where are you going?"

"I don't know exactly. I just take it one day at a time. I just want to be happy."

"And what is happiness for you, Maggie?"

"For so many years, it was making sure my kids were happy. But, for all practical purposes, they are adults now. So here I am without David, my children gone, trying to discover or rediscover the real Maggie McWilliams."

"You and I have an advantage over a lot of people, Maggie: our age."

"I don't know that growing older is an advantage."

"Sure it is. We are in our best years."

"How so when I just feel old? The kids at my university look at me like I'm ancient," Maggie said.

"This age is the best because we are mature enough to have confidence in ourselves. We are comfortable in our own skin. We know what we will put up with and what we won't tolerate. Financially, we have had our best years."

Maggie wondered if she should tell Sam about her financial situation. She didn't want to scare him or make him feel pity for her. She was barely living from month to month, from paycheck to paycheck. David had left some debt, and Maggie was barely keeping her head above water. She didn't know what was worse: being alone or wondering if someone was going to come and put a padlock on her front door someday. The idea of filing for bankruptcy scared her to death. Maggie knew people could be employed one month and then living on the streets three months later.

"Keep talking, Sam. You almost have me convinced."

"Besides, you are more beautiful now than ever."

"Come on, Sam. I was definitely more attractive at eighteen."

"No way. Now your eyes sparkle with great insight. You are beautiful outside, but you are much more beautiful inside."

"I need to keep you around. You may think I'm beautiful, but just ask the person who colors my hair every six weeks. She can tell you I'm covering up a lot of gray."

"I've had a lot more time than you to think about these things."

"Sometimes I feel like I've wasted my life since David died."

"Why?"

"I don't know exactly. It's just a feeling. I haven't done much except think."

"It takes time to process these things, Maggie. I'm not one to read self-help books, but I read a book a few years ago that made a profound impact on my life. It said that if you waste the first half of your life, that's okay, because you are young and that is what most of us do, but if you waste the second half of your life, then shame on you because you should know better. And that's what you are doing. You are trying to figure out the second half of your life."

"Did you read that book before or after you went to Brazil?"

"Before, but I didn't come to fully understand it until I lived in Brazil. At first, it was dumb luck—and a little guidance from God—that sent me to cover that soccer championship in Rio. I discovered a lot of people in Brazil have so little, but they still have hope. Amazingly enough, they have never lost hope. They taught me so much."

"Do you wish you could go back to Brazil?"

Sam knew that was a loaded question. Being a missionary in Brazil had been an important part of his life. It had definitely been the most meaningful, if not the most rewarding, three years he had inhabited the earth. "Being a missionary, well, it's hard to explain. You feel so free. You wake up each morning, and you only have one thing on your mind: How can I help someone today? There are no deadlines, no corporate executives to impress, no ratings to improve, and no benchmarks to eclipse. It's a good feeling to serve others."

How could Maggie ever consider taking Sam away from his new life, a life that been so fulfilling? If Sam left Brazil for good and wasn't happy, Maggie could never forgive herself. And there is no way she would ever live in South America. "When do you have to return, Sam?"

"I don't have to return. It's up in the air. Right now, it's not on my mind. Being right here with you at the lake on a beautiful day is all that matters to me." Sam turned on his side and inched close to Maggie. He slid his hand across her waist and drew her closer. Without another word, Sam pressed his lips to hers. Maggie's lips were full and moist. She tasted like honeysuckle in the spring.

That kiss led to another, then another, and each time, Maggie and Sam would press a little closer together, each one growing in intensity. It had been a long time since either Maggie or Sam had been so excited.

After a deep breath, Maggie climbed on top of Sam, her legs straddling his waist. She couldn't help but think that he was in great shape for a man closing in on sixty. "I've got you right where I want you, mister."

"And where would that be?"

"Right here with me—even if it is only for a short time."

"Who says it has to be a short time?"

"I say."

"And who are you to tell me what to do with my life?"

Even when he jokes, Sam is tender, Maggie thought. *His genteel nature is very seductive. Without much encouragement, I could easily become spoiled by this man.* "From my perspective, it looks like I'm in charge right now, doesn't it?"

"You do have a point. I don't mind you being in charge. Whatever you say, dear."

"Stop it—or I'll never let you get up."

Sam made a sudden shift, trying to throw Maggie to the side.

"Now you've done it." Maggie took his arms and pinned them behind his head. Of course, she couldn't have done it without some help from Sam. Now that she had him, Maggie didn't know what to do next. She didn't have to wait long to find out.

Sam pulled her down close to him.

This time, it was her turn to kiss him. She pressed hard, and she seemed to melt right into his body. Maggie could easily tell Sam was hard from head to toe. She could feel the excitement. Even at her age, she thought it was amazing that a man wanted to be with her, hold her, and love her.

Maggie couldn't get enough of Sam at the moment. She was afraid to open her eyes, afraid the moment would vanish, afraid Sam would vanish. She was afraid she would awaken from a dream—a dream of contentment, of longing, of fulfillment.

Maggie wanted Sam to take her clothes off right then and there. She didn't care who was looking or what might happen to them. She wanted Sam to make love to her by the water's edge. She wanted him to make her feel like she had never felt before, never dared dream of feeling. Maggie was ready to throw caution to the wind. All she wanted at that moment was Sam's body and his love.

Sam ran his fingers through Maggie's hair as he kissed her cheek. In an instant, he flipped her over. Now he was on top of her. Everything in him told him he wanted her at that moment. He could tell she wanted him, but timing was everything. No matter how much Sam had dreamed of a scene like that, he had never really allowed himself to imagine it would happen. He wanted Maggie, but it had to be the right time and in the right way. "I don't think I can take much more of this." He moved to her side. "I mean, I could, but I can't. Do you follow any of that?"

"I'll give you permission to keep going," Maggie said through her big smile.

"It would be so easy, but I want it to happen for the right reason at the right time."

"You understand there are only three or four men in the world who would say no at a time like this?"

"It's going to happen soon enough," Sam said. "I just don't want to be arrested. I can see the headlines now: 'Elderly Couple Arrested for Having Sex at the Lake.' That would make Lucy and Lily proud of their mom. Call me old-fashioned, but I just want it to be on our honeymoon with a harvest moon and champagne."

"You are a romantic like I've never witnessed, Sam Roberts."

"Guilty as charged, especially when I'm with you. You and I will know when the time is right."

"But I want to take advantage of you while I have you. I don't want to waste another minute. We can go back to my house and, you know …"

"Have sex?"

"Yes, passionate, sweaty, I'm-too-tired-to-move-a-muscle sex."

"Patience is a virtue, Maggie. You keep thinking I'm going somewhere else when I'm not. I'm right here."

"You are going somewhere else—Brazil—and I'm not going to stop you."

"If I want to go to Brazil, I'll go. Don't worry. Right now, I want to be here with you in beautiful Natchitoches, Louisiana."

"I still can't quite get my head around that notion."

"That I want to be with you in Natchitoches?"

"Just a minute ago, I could feel you wanted to be with me."

"I want to be with you in Natchitoches, or Los Angeles, or New York, or London, or Calcutta. It doesn't matter to me."

"That's hard to believe, Sam," Maggie said, getting up on her knees. "You've already told me the place does matter. Brazil does matter. That little town where you lived does matter. The people there do matter."

Sam could tell the conversation was moving in the

wrong direction. What he was trying to say was that he could live anywhere—as long as Maggie was there. He could easily live in Natchitoches, if that's what she wanted. Grow where you are planted, right? His world revolved around Maggie—and not the other way around. "My time in Brazil does matter, but it pales compared to what I feel for you. I've thought about you for many more years than I've been with the people in my little village."

Maggie couldn't help but laugh. "We've been together a few months in our entire lives. That sounds insane, but it's true. We were together a few months as teenagers, and now a whole forty-eight hours."

"You've been with me in spirit ever since I met you. I just believe I know all I need to know to make this work."

"I refuse to let you give up on your missionary work that easily," Maggie said. "You have to go back there."

"Why do we have to talk about this now?"

"Because it's important, Sam. What if you moved here, and in two years, you were unhappy. I could never forgive myself. You would have to start all over with me. It's just too much to ask."

Sam could tell Maggie wasn't going to give up on this conversation—and he just had to hang in there the best he could. "Please stop trying to figure out my life for me. Are you trying to sabotage this relationship?"

That statement took Maggie by surprise. *A relationship?* Sam said they had a relationship. Until that moment, she had not thought about she and Sam having a full-blown, honest-to-goodness *relationship*. She liked the way the word fit just right. "Then, where do we go from here?"

"How about dinner tonight? You know, when you are our age, everything revolves around food. If you don't mind, allow me to make all the arrangements. I know that isn't very twenty-first-century thinking, but, just this once, I would like to take care of all the details."

"You mean like a we-are-dating-each-other-exclusively date?"

"Like that. I promise to have you home by curfew."

"I meant to ask you, Sam, what kind of food do you like best—besides Brazilian cuisine?"

"Any kind really: Italian, Mexican, Asian."

"How about my favorite—a cheeseburger with fries?"

"So you still like cheeseburgers. That's surprising since you still have that girlish figure."

"Don't forget the shake."

"Chocolate. Right?"

"Great memory."

"It sounds like the perfect meal to me, Maggie."

As they were gathering their things to head back to the

city, Sam said, "There's one more thing I want to talk to you about, Maggie."

"Sure."

"I would like to stay another day, if that meets with your approval. We'll call it a three-day weekend."

"Keep going. It sounds like there is a method to your madness."

"There is. If you can stand it, I'll make all the arrangements tomorrow, as well."

"I don't mind cooking for us, Sam."

"No, I have something special in mind. It's my turn. You've done much more cooking over the past twenty years or so. Let me have a go at it."

"Are you cooking?"

"No way, but I promise to try to make it memorable."

"I love surprises—at least the good kind of surprises. Then, are you going to leave?"

"I'm having a great time. I don't want to leave, but the plan is to leave in a couple of days."

"I'll miss you."

"I was hoping you would say that, Maggie."

Sam was planning to return to Brazil in forty-eight hours—and he wanted Maggie on that plane with him. He just had to figure out how to make it happen.

Chapter 10

Maggie's stomach was fluttering—and not in a good way. She felt a little down. The thought of Sam leaving and returning to Brazil left a hole in her stomach. It was selfish, but she didn't want him to go.

Maggie didn't know what to do.

Falling in love at her age seemed like an odd thing somehow, but why? Love isn't bound by age or gender or time or space. Perhaps she was discovering a new kind of love. A deeper, more meaningful love.

At first, Maggie fought her feelings. It was natural, she convinced herself, but letting go was even more natural, she reasoned, because she would only be at peace if she could feel with her heart instead of her head.

Like Sam said, love is without motivation or condition. Certainly, her feelings blossomed because Sam rang her doorbell on Friday afternoon.

For two years, Maggie had buried her feelings. It was strictly survival mode. Wake up, teach, eat, sleep, repeat. Wake up, teach, eat, sleep, repeat. When she was around Lily and Lucy, Maggie had to make sure she could fake it. The only trouble was she was still faking it.

Sam had changed her rhythm for the better. Maggie's intuition told her this was the type of love that could grow day by day, the type of love that would allow her to receive and not only give. It was the kind of love that would allow her to wake every morning knowing that no matter what happened, it was going to be a good day because Sam was in her life.

Why would she ever let someone this special leave? Why not ask him to stay? He said he would stay another day or two. Why not? Maybe a day would turn into a week, and that would turn into a month, and a month could easily become a year. And a year could turn into forever.

Feelings so special that it hurts don't happen every day, Maggie thought. *There has to be a way to keep Sam in Natchitoches. If he gets back on that plane and heads to Brazil, I will probably never see him again.* She didn't want to let that happen.

"You're awfully quiet," Sam said over the smooth jazz station playing on his rental car's satellite radio. "A penny for your thoughts? How about a dollar for your thoughts?"

Maggie didn't know what to say, and she decided a little white lie wouldn't hurt anything. "I'm just thinking about all the things I have to do before I start the new semester."

"And you've got some land in Florida you want to sell me?" Sam couldn't help the sarcasm. "What were you really thinking?"

"About us." Maggie hoped that would be enough for Sam.

"That I do believe. I also believe you were thinking deep thoughts, but I'm not going to interrogate you. When the time is right, I know you will share."

"I'm excited about dinner—even if I don't know where we are going." Maggie knew it was a bit shifty, but she wasn't lying. She was excited about dinner.

"Five more minutes, and we will be at our destination," Sam said in his best navigator voice.

Sam wheeled into a tight parking spot next to the Cane River boat dock and turned off the key. He quickly slid out of his seat, went to Maggie's side of the car, and opened her door.

"It's been a long time since anyone has opened my door for me," Maggie said. "But, Sam, there aren't any restaurants around here."

Sam took Maggie by the hand and led her down the boat dock. In just a couple of minutes, Maggie and Sam were standing in front of the *River Runner*. The thirty-foot river cruiser had seen her share of tourists over the years, but she still had plenty of life in her.

"We are going on a cruise?" Maggie asked.

"A dinner cruise," Sam replied. "A sunset dinner cruise, to be precise."

Just then, a man dressed in a blue and white sailor's cap, a white T-shirt, and jeans jumped from the *River Runner* to the dock. "Mr. Roberts?"

"Yes, I'm Sam Roberts."

"Welcome aboard, sir. I'm Captain Wilson, but you can call me Randy. In fact, just about everyone calls me Captain Randy."

"Well, Captain Randy, allow me to introduce Maggie. Maggie, Captain Randy."

"Have we met, Miss Maggie?" The captain gave Maggie a quizzical look.

"I don't think so. I've always wanted to take this cruise, but I just never got around to it. My girls begged me to do this, but life gets busy."

Two years ago, the captain's comment wouldn't have meant anything to Maggie, but since the death of her husband, Maggie was a little sensitive about any question or offhand comments that came her way. *Some might even say I'm a little paranoid. Just another thing to work on in the future,* Maggie thought.

"It's good to have you with us this evening," Captain Randy said. Turning to Sam, he added, "Everything is prepared as you wished, Mr. Roberts."

Maggie thought, *I wonder what that means.*

Sam took Maggie's hand once again, and with Captain Randy's help, they went aboard the *River Runner.*

"We will be shoving off in just a few minutes, Mr. Roberts," the captain said.

Maggie turned to Sam and said, "Aren't we waiting for more people to come on the cruise?"

The captain jumped in and said, "It's just the two of you." He walked to the other end of the *River Runner* and gave the order to push away from the dock.

"Sam, what is this?" Every photo Maggie had ever seen showed a large group of tourists and locals on the boat as it cruised up and down the Cane River.

"I just thought we could share a quiet meal tonight. Nothing fancy. I got the idea when we were at the Landing. There was a brochure, and the tourist bureau must have done a good job because here we are. Remember when I went back into the kitchen for so long before we left? I was making all the catering arrangements then."

Sam is pretty sure of himself, Maggie thought. "Just us on the boat, dinner, and a cruise. That must cost you a pretty penny."

"Why do you think I said a penny for your thoughts?"

"Seriously, Sam. This is exactly what I'm talking about—you with no job, spending this kind of money. I didn't think you were that irresponsible."

"Truce. It's going to be okay. I promise. Can't we just enjoy the evening and each other?"

Maggie felt a slight jerk as the *River Runner* pulled away from the dock. *No reason to fight it*, Maggie thought. The boat was moving, and there was no going back. She might as well trust Sam and enjoy a quiet evening on the Cane River.

The chug-a-chug of the boat was soothing, and the evening breeze was welcome—even if it tousled Maggie's hair.

Sam took Maggie to the bow of the boat to get a better view of the river and the sun, which was setting rapidly. *It's too bad this beautiful, red ball makes the temperature feel like an oven warming to four hundred degrees. Thank goodness*, Maggie thought, *the canopy can take a little of the sting out of the heat and humidity*. Maggie suddenly understood why Sam had told her to wear a pair of colored jeans and a sleeveless blouse to dinner. She loved her colored jeans, especially the ones she had on this evening. They were baby blue—it was no coincidence they matched Sam's eyes. Her white knit polo was the perfect choice for this particular evening.

Sam looked just as stunning in his short-sleeved, light green dress shirt and off-white, almost tan, linen pants. Maggie should have guessed where they were going when Sam slipped on his brown leather boat shoes.

"Your favorite drink, ma'am," Captain Randy said, handing Maggie a Diet Dr Pepper. "I have one for you, too, Mr. Roberts."

"Just call me Sam."

"Yes, sir. We are preparing your dinner now, and it will be ready in about twenty minutes. In the meantime, please enjoy the Landing's signature spinach and artichoke dip."

"Looks wonderful," Maggie said, "but I probably won't be hungry if I eat all this."

"I'll be happy to help," Sam said with a smile.

For the next few minutes, Maggie and Sam sat near the front of the *River Runner*, nibbling on chips and dip, sipping their drinks, and quietly enjoying the view.

It didn't seem like twenty minutes, but Captain Randy soon returned and said that dinner was served.

"What's on the menu this evening?" Maggie asked.

"I honestly have no idea," Sam said. "I just told the chef to make something special for you. I can eat almost anything."

At the back of the boat, a small table was set with a white tablecloth, a vase of freshly cut gardenias, fine china, crystal, and silverware. Soft music was playing in the background. Even though it was recorded, having love songs playing in the background was a nice touch.

When the first course came, Maggie and Sam were impressed. It was a small walnut, cranberry, and goat cheese salad with balsamic vinaigrette dressing. Light and flavorful, it was perfect for a summer evening.

The main course was chicken, lightly breaded, sauteed in butter, and served in lemon butter with a demi-glace sauce. It came with a small side of pasta—just the right amount.

"I don't know if I have room for dessert, but I know it's coming," Sam said.

"Maybe we could split it." Maggie had always had a sweet tooth.

"I want to talk with you about a serious subject," Sam said.

"I'm listening," Maggie said. "Besides, we are on the river. Where could I possibly go? I can't swim to shore from here. It's too dark—even with this beautiful moon."

"I want you to marry me, Maggie."

"You don't waste any time, do you?"

"I mean it. I really want you to think about it, but don't take too long."

"One minute you say I can take my time with this 'relationship,' as you call it, and the next minute, you want an answer. I don't know what to think."

"I know it's a crazy time for both of us. We've both led very different lives, but here we are. I know you care about me, and you know how much I care about you."

"Are you insisting on an answer tonight, Sam?"

"I would never insist."

"Good. Allow me to rephrase the question: Would you prefer an answer tonight?"

"You've promised me another day tomorrow. How about we compromise and say tomorrow?"

"How is that a compromise? How about if I promise to think about it overnight, and if the answer is yes, I'll tell you tomorrow. If I say no, or if I can't decide, then we will just have to see what happens next. That is the best I can do."

"I'm sorry, Maggie. Forgive me. No more high-pressure sales pitches, I promise."

What am I thinking? I want Sam to stay. I don't want him to leave, but I want to make the right decision for myself and the girls. This is a delicate balancing act. Even at fifty-eight years of age and all of my life experiences, I still don't know what do when it comes to Sam. "Tomorrow, then."

"Tomorrow," Sam repeated.

Maggie didn't know what she would ultimately tell Sam, but she had bought herself another twenty-four hours. *Maybe I will wake up on Monday morning—and the answer will come to me. No pressure. It's just the biggest decision of my life.*

Part IV

Monday Morning

Chapter 11

"When were you going to tell me?"

For a moment, Sam was stunned by Maggie's question. This was not the way he wanted to start the day. "Tell you what?"

"Or maybe you weren't planning on telling me at all." Maggie's voice was getting higher.

"Tell you what?" Sam's voice was rising to the same level of exasperation.

"You haven't been honest with me. Why didn't you tell me that you paid for my girls' so-called scholarships to LSU?"

"I've tried to be honest with you, Maggie. Maybe we could sit outside on your deck and talk about it."

Sam needed a moment to collect his thoughts, and the best way for him to buy time was getting Maggie from her living room to her backyard. Yes, he did pay for the last three years the twins went to college, but he never thought anyone would ever find out. "It was an anonymous gift," Sam said. "Who told you?"

Maggie was visibly shaken, but she was trying her best to hold her composure. Only one thought ran through her mind: *Another man with another secret.* "Lucy called me this morning, and the twins rarely call me two days in a row. I knew something was wrong. Lucy told me she was talking with a sorority sister who works in administration at LSU. Lucy told her friend that you came to see me. When Lucy's friend heard your name, she was taken aback. She told Lucy you were the one who paid for the twins' tuition, books, and room and board. Everything. Is it true?"

Sam hesitated. "Yes, it's true."

"It was wrong for Lucy's friend to disclose that type of information, but she did it anyway because she believed Lucy had a right to know. She could be fired if you wanted to make a big deal out of it."

"I don't want to make a big deal out of it—with LSU or with you. I really never thought anyone would know I made that donation."

"You pay for my children's college education, not to mention room and board, and you don't think it's a big deal?"

"Not at the time. I can see it is now."

"Don't you think you should have asked me first?"

"It was a scholarship."

"Was anyone else eligible for the scholarship?"

"Not really, no, but ..."

"But what?"

"I wanted to do it for you. If I would have asked first, what would you have said? What would your husband have said? What would your husband have thought?"

"I would have said no. Thanks, but no thanks.'"

"I understand, but why?"

"Two reasons. First, David and I could afford to send Lucy and Lily to college. It would have been a stretch, but we could have done it. Yes, the girls may have had small loans to pay back, but that's pretty typical these days. Secondly, how would I have explained you to David? Frankly, it's a little weird, don't you think?"

"I had a little extra money at the time, and I thought I would help out."

"I made sure Lucy and Lily applied for scholarships, but we never expected they would get full scholarships. When they came through, we didn't ask too many questions. Looking back, I guess we should have asked a lot of questions."

"The twins were smart, and I didn't give them anything they didn't deserve."

"Like all moms, I was blind when it came to the twins. I knew they did pretty well in high school, but not that well. You know what they say, if something is too good to be true, then it probably is."

"I'm sorry, Maggie. I would never have done it if I thought it was going to be a problem."

"I'm not sure an apology is enough."

"I hope we can somehow get past this, Maggie."

"I don't know. I honestly don't know."

"Meaning?"

"Meaning I have this little problem trusting men these days. Starting with my former husband. I put all my trust in him—and look what happened—and now you."

"With all due respect, please don't put me in the same category with your former husband. I thought I was doing something positive to help you. David did a destructive thing, if I may be so blunt."

Maggie couldn't hold back the tears any longer. She buried her face in her hands and began to sob, her body shaking slightly.

Sam moved to put his arms around her.

They sat in silence for a few minutes until she could begin to regain her composure.

"I never met the girl David assaulted. It wasn't her fault. She trusted an adult—and see where that got her? She had every right to come forward, to go to the police. I hope she is doing better, I really do, but what David did to her will never go away. She will live with it for the rest of her life."

"You do know that what David did is not your fault." Sam didn't know what else to say.

"It's my fault for being so stupid. It's my fault for not seeing the signs. Some sign. Honestly, we had an average marriage. Not great, but not bad. We weren't madly in love, but how many people are after so many years of marriage?"

"I've loved you for all these years, and I've never grown tired of it."

"You didn't have to live with me. And I didn't live with you. It would have been a totally different dynamic."

Yes, Sam thought. *It would have been a different dynamic, but I wouldn't have taken advantage of a fourteen-year-old girl. And Maggie and the twins wouldn't have had to live with their husband and dad committing suicide. David changed a teenager's life forever, and he compounded the problem by changing the lives of his wife and children forever. That's what suicide does to a family. Of course, the person committing suicide is so ill mentally he or she never realizes what will happen to those left behind. No, Maggie and I wouldn't have had a perfect marriage—we certainly would have had our ups and downs, but comparatively speaking, I am sure we would have had a solid marriage built on love and respect.*

"I was the dutiful little wife. Maybe I should have tried harder. I thought about it a million times. What could I have done differently? I don't know. I know I feel guilty because I didn't try harder."

"What David did was about David—not you. Of course, I'm biased. It's going to take time, but you and the girls can get past this. If you don't, it's going to drive you crazy. Literally. Then what good will you be for Lucy and Lily? They need you."

"I know. I can see it in their eyes, and I can hear it in their voices. I'm all they have left. Sometimes I know they worry I will die too. They don't want to be orphans at such a young age, even though they are adults."

"You have to keep working to get better. You have to do it for them. And there's another reason. *Me.* I need you."

"You have gotten along fine without me all these years. You don't need anyone."

"That's not true. I need you, Maggie. I'm this close to you now. I don't want to let you go. I want to help. I want to be there for you. I don't know how many times or ways I can say I'm sorry for any problem I caused by giving Lucy and Lily those scholarships."

"Sam, I want you to understand where I'm coming from on this. I don't know if I should get married again. I don't know if my children can picture me with anyone else."

"I don't know Lucy and Lily. I've just met them, but I would think they want you to be happy. I believe—I know—I can make you happy. Look at this weekend. Tell me you haven't been happy."

"I have been happy. Very happy, but that is beside the point."

"Then, what is the point?"

"I have so much baggage, and so do you. If we are going to be honest, I'm getting mixed signals from you too, Sam. One minute, you want to spend the rest of your life with me. The next minute, you are flying back to Brazil. You know, I thought you were perfect. I couldn't find a flaw. Then I discovered you aren't prefect. Far from perfect. In fact, you may be a coward. Maybe you are really trying to tell me subliminally that this is too much for you."

"Damn it, Maggie. I don't know what else to say to you. I've made my best case for us being together. You have to decide what you want to do."

"Where do we go from here?"

"How did you leave it with the twins this morning?"

"They told me the same thing—if I want to be with you, they will support me. They just wanted me to know about the scholarships. Ultimately, they were glad not to have any debt coming out of college."

"So we can have a truce?"

"Truce."

"Besides, you promised we could have today. Do you need some time to get ready so we can go?"

"Are you telling me I don't look so hot right now?"

"I just thought you might need a little time."

"Where are we going, Sam?"

"That's my secret."

"Please, no more secrets."

"Just one more. I promise you will like it. At least, I'm hoping so. I would ask you to trust me one more time, but I've been using that trust word too much lately."

"Give me thirty minutes to change and freshen up, and I'll be ready to go."

"And I'm not a coward. I'm ready to marry you right now. You just have to say yes." Sam was relieved to get past another major hurdle with Maggie. He was hoping it was the last one. *I'm not a coward, and I am about to prove it.*

While Maggie was getting ready in her bedroom, Sam thought about their weekend together. It had been the best weekend of his life. As good as it had been to see Maggie, he couldn't help but think about the future. *What will happen in the next two days? Two years? Two decades? Sometimes it's difficult when a fantasy becomes a reality. Sometimes the fantasy*

is easier than facing reality. The fantasy can be put in a nice, neat place. You know where it is at all times. You control it. Reality is much more difficult. It requires a risk. It requires an investment in emotions. As that bumper sticker says, 'Stuff happens.' And when stuff happens, you have to be ready to bend like a willow.

The Maggie in his mind and heart was one thing. He could handle that easily. He had for years. Now he could touch her, kiss her, hold her. He could tell her his feelings. She could tell him her feelings.

Sure, the risk was much greater now. In his fantasy, Maggie was always perfect. He was always perfect. In some ways, she was still the eighteen-year-old he had fallen in love with all those years ago. She was still the little princess in a French twist and red evening dress.

The Maggie of the present was better. Much better. He liked Maggie at fifty-eight much better than the Maggie of eighteen. She was still beautiful, but she had a deeper inner quality. Even with all the tragedy in her life, Maggie had a deeper sense of self.

"I'm ready," she announced, breezing into the room.

"You look beautiful, as always," Sam responded.

"Are you sure I'm not underdressed? Are you sure I can wear a pair of pants and this top?"

"Positive."

"I am curious about where we are going. If it's a really nice restaurant, I can't go like this."

"I promise. Trust me."

"There you go with that trust thing again."

"So will you trust me one last time?"

"I'm going, aren't I?"

"I guess that answers my question."

With that, Sam opened the car door for Maggie, and she slid into the passenger seat. In minutes, they were headed north on the interstate to Shreveport. For most of the trip, they rode in silence. To Sam, that was a good sign. At that moment, at least, they didn't have to fill each moment with idle chatter because they were so comfortable with each other. Sam thought that maybe sometime between Friday afternoon and Monday afternoon, they had become a couple.

"We are like an old married couple," Sam said, breaking the silence.

"What do you mean?"

"We really haven't spoken to each other since we got in the car."

"I've been wondering where we are going." *I'm pretty familiar with the restaurants in Shreveport, but why drive an hour for lunch?*

"We are like an old pair of shoes," Sam said, ignoring

Maggie's remark. "You keep them forever because they are so comfortable."

They both laughed. Maggie knew it was true. She could be open with Sam. And she did want to trust him more than anything. It didn't hurt that he was drop-dead gorgeous. No doubt, he had that made-for-television persona. And he was nicer than nice.

"What's the name of the restaurant—maybe I've heard of it," Maggie asked.

"I doubt it."

"How can you be so sure. I've lived in northwest Louisiana for too many years not to know a good bit about its culture. Shreveport may be an hour from Natchitoches, but I've been there more than a few times."

"You don't know this one."

"Give me a pop test then."

"Always the professor. Okay, it's called Oceanside."

"The name of the restaurant in Shreveport, which is nowhere near the ocean, is called Oceanside? It must be new." *Funny name for a restaurant in Shreveport*, Maggie thought. *Maybe the gimmick is to make customers think they are at the ocean. Not a bad idea. So many people love the beach. I certainly do.*

"Now I'm really confused," Maggie said Sam drove through downtown Shreveport and headed northwest, passing a sign that pointed them toward the downtown airport. "There aren't any good restaurants this way, much less one called Oceanside."

Sam didn't respond. He kept his mind on the airport signs. In a few minutes, he passed the main entrance to the airport. It was a typical public-use facility, dotted with private planes. Sam parked, opened Maggie's door, and ushered her inside before she could say a word.

At the nearest counter, the attendant looked up from her computer. "Good morning. May I help you?"

"Yes, I'm Sam Roberts."

The attendant went back to her computer screen, and then she looked up with a wide smile. "Thank you, Mr. Roberts."

"Sam, what in the world are we doing?"

"We are going to skip lunch—at least a formal lunch—and have dinner. You did say you would have dinner with me, didn't you?"

"Yes, but … could you let me think for just a minute?"

Sam looked at Maggie, then at the airline attendant, then back at Maggie. He didn't say a thing as he waited for Maggie to make the next move.

"Tell me why we are at the downtown Shreveport airport."

"We are here because I have a plane waiting for us."

"And why is there a plane waiting for us?"

"To take us to dinner."

"This is like pulling teeth. Why do we need a plane to take us to dinner? I thought we were going to a restaurant named Oceanside in Shreveport."

"I never said that. I only said we were going to eat at a place called Oceanside."

"So we aren't going to eat in Shreveport? Where are we going to have dinner?"

"That is my surprise. It's going to be great. Let go for once. Do something new and different. I wouldn't put you in a compromising situation. You do know that, don't you?"

"Are we coming back tonight?"

"If you want to come back tonight, we can. If you want to stay over, we can do that, too."

"The kids have no idea where I will be."

"Did you bring your cell phone with you?"

"Sure."

"Do they ever call that number?"

"All the time."

"Remember, do you know where they are every minute of the day?"

"No, and that's why a mother worries all the time, but I get your point. They have their own lives now. Okay, we better get going before I change my mind."

Sam wanted to keep his plan a secret from Maggie. He wanted to unravel his top-secret excursion bit by bit. *So far, so good.*

"Right through Gate A," the attendant said, motioning them to the back of the terminal.

A sleek, white Learjet was no more than twenty-five yards from the gate. The engines were running, which meant that Maggie couldn't hear Sam as he mouthed the words "Follow me."

The pilot was in his early forties, and he greeted Sam with a firm handshake and a warm smile. He extended his hand to Maggie, and then he helped her up the narrow stairs that led into the aircraft. Sam was right behind her.

The jet was cozy and comfortable, but above all, it was elegant. Maggie had never been on a small jet, much less flown in one. The Lear had enough seating to accommodate a dozen passengers, but today, it would only have two. To the rear of the plane, there was a small dining table that could double as a work area for busy executives. Maggie could tell the pale blue cotton curtains on the windows had been custom-made.

Maggie had seen photos of Learjets. Because pop culture was so prevalent in the twenty-first century, she had seen celebrities on television jetting off to faraway islands for vacations. *This is a great way to fly,* she thought. *No waiting.*

No luggage to check. No metal detectors. Plenty of space to stretch out. Yes, this is how the rich and famous go from New York to Paris and from Los Angeles to Hawaii. This isn't how a professor and mother of two goes to dinner. She was determined not to ask any more questions, even though she had a million of them racing through her brain. She was determined just to enjoy the ride. And Sam.

A few minutes after they fastened their safety belts, the plane began to taxi toward the runway. Maggie gave Sam one of her best smiles, hoping he couldn't detect all the nervous energy she felt.

Maggie looks like a little girl in a candy store, Sam thought.

"Sam, you shouldn't have," Maggie said. "You don't have to impress me like this. Besides, you don't even have a job right now. This has got to cost a lot of money."

Sam couldn't help but laugh out loud. With that, the Learjet was in the air with more power than Maggie imagined—like a Roman candle shooting toward the stars. Maggie felt a rush of adrenaline, even though she had no clue where the Lear—or her life—was headed.

Chapter 12

"I don't know where we are, but we have to be in the United States," Maggie said as she descended the steps of the Learjet. "When are you going to give me another clue, Sam?"

For the ninety-minute trip, Sam made sure he and Maggie engaged in small talk. He wanted to keep her mind occupied as much as possible. Sam didn't want to spoil his big surprise.

As much as she wanted to ask, Maggie played the game and literally went along for the ride.

There was a vehicle and driver waiting for them no more than a hundred feet from where the Lear came to a final stop. "What, no limo?" Maggie joked, staring at a fully-restored 1985 Jeep Grand Wagoneer.

"Maggie, say hello to Jack," Sam said, ignoring Maggie's quip. "Jack, this is Maggie."

Jack touched the bill of his old fishing cap and nodded to Maggie. "Nice to meet you, Maggie. I've heard a lot of great things about you."

"I think Sam is slightly prejudiced, but thank you, Jack."

As Sam and Maggie slipped into the backseat of the vintage station wagon, Sam took Maggie's hand in his, just to reassure her everything was going to be all right.

"We have timed this just about right, I think," Sam said to Jack. "We have just the right amount of daylight left."

"And what does daylight have to do with dinner at the Oceanside restaurant?" Maggie wanted to know. She also wanted to know how Sam knew Jack, or how Jack knew Sam, but Maggie had to wait to ask that question.

"Patience, my dear. All will be revealed in good time. Would you mind if we listened to some music?"

Before Maggie could answer, Sam asked Jack to play some soft jazz. He chose an instrumental disc by jazz pianist Keiko Matsui. The gentle melodies flowed through the vehicle.

Maggie began to feel a little tired from all that day's activities, and she closed her eyes for a moment to collect her thoughts. She must have dozed off for a few minutes because she felt her head jerk when the Grand Wagoneer rolled to a stop.

"I'm sorry, Sam. How long did I sleep? I must have been more tired than I realized."

"No need to apologize. I took the opportunity to shut my eyes for just a minute, too. If anything, both of us should apologize to Jack."

Jack gave a familiar tip of his cap.

Maggie looked up to see a sky blue beach house that dwarfed their vehicle. The beauty of the house was only eclipsed, Maggie thought, by the fact that it was on the water.

"Oh, my God, Sam. What a beautiful house!"

"I'm glad you like it," Sam said, opening the door so Maggie could get out. "I can't wait to give you a tour."

Maggie raced up the steps, which led to a wraparound deck. She wanted to take a minute to watch the waves dancing onto the shore. "You remembered how much I love the ocean, didn't you, Sam?"

"When it comes to you, I don't forget very much." Sam was right behind her, and he put his hands around her waist. They stared at the blue-green water in silence.

"I'd like to see the house now," Maggie said like a child on Christmas morning.

Walking inside, Sam said, "This is the great room."

"I know, silly."

The great room was just that—great. It was large and

comfortable. The wall facing the ocean was glass from floor to ceiling. And the ceiling had to be twelve feet tall. The other walls, covered with art from several different genres, were a crisp off-white, which blended perfectly with the blond wood floors. There also was a fireplace with a small stack of wood.

Across the room was a dining table with eight chairs—cozy enough for intimate dinners, but functional enough to host additional guests. Maggie loved the rustic wood table and dark green chairs.

The kitchen was large and modern with stainless steel appliances, an industrial gas stove, and a large island in the middle. The light gray granite countertops blended nicely with the gray and white cabinets. A stainless ceiling pot rack was filled with Cuisinart cookware. A cast-iron skillet was on the stove.

There was a second fireplace in the master bedroom, which was on the south end of the house. The walls, which were the same off-white, were covered with photographs from around the world. All the photos were black and white, but that was all they had in common. Some were landscapes, some were people, and some captured famous sites, like the Eiffel Tower or the Vatican. The room was tastefully done with a contemporary king-sized bed, two modern nightstands, and matching brass table lamps. An antique armoire, finished in a gunmetal gray, was against the far wall.

The master bath was just as stunning with its glass, walk-in shower, and standalone tub, complete with Jacuzzi jets. The light fixtures continued the contemporary theme, and there was plenty of counter space with double sinks.

The closet was almost as big as a bedroom, and there were tons of extras, from roll-out storage baskets and shoe racks to a retractable dressing mirror and a fold-out ironing board.

On the north side of the home, Maggie found another full bath, which was tastefully decorated with contemporary accents. Next to the bathroom was a small study that was filled with books and a computer on a sleek desk with matching chair.

Upstairs, there were three bedrooms and three baths. Each bedroom and bath could be closed off, much like a bed-and-breakfast. One bedroom had art from southern painter Clementine Hunter, and another bedroom had art by Kevin Berlin. The third bedroom was filled with art showcasing ocean scenes.

The outside deck had plenty of room for a table with umbrella, chairs, and matching lounge chairs with bright yellow cushions.

"What a beautiful house. Someone has good taste," Maggie said.

"There's something else we need to do before we begin our big evening," Sam said. "We need to take you shopping."

"Time out, Sam. I have a million questions for you first."

"Okay, shoot."

"Where are we?" Maggie knew it sounded like a dumb question as soon as she asked it.

"We are in Florida. Destin, to be exact. My favorite beach in the world. My parents never liked the beach, so this was never an option, but I discovered it quite by accident years ago. I had to do an interview with an up-and-coming professional golfer, and she would only give me the time if I came to her parents' beach home in Destin. I immediately fell in love with Destin."

"Who is Jack?"

"He's a friend."

"And?"

"And he takes care of this beach house."

"And?"

"Yes, this house belongs to me."

"I'm starting to get a new view of you, Sam. Is that your jet, too?"

"No, unfortunately, it's not. It's part of a fleet, and I just leased it for this trip."

"Either you have a lot of money—or you are going to be asking me for a loan pretty soon. I don't know which just yet." Maggie hated to discuss finances, but that didn't stop her. She figured she had the right, especially if she and Sam became permanent. She didn't want to support a deadbeat, although Sam seemed like anything but a con artist, but didn't all great con artists seem legitimate?

"I don't want to talk about money right now, if that is all right with you, Maggie."

"We have to have that talk sooner or later, Sam."

"That's a deal, just not now. Okay?"

"Okay for now."

"Jack left his car for us. Let's freshen up and go shopping. Are you hungry? We can get a bite on the way to the outlet mall."

As they drove down scenic Highway 98, Destin was as beautiful as Maggie had imagined. She and the twins loved to holiday in Gulf Shores, but David never did. A lot of tourists would go to Gulf Shores in Alabama, and Maggie was one of them. She had never thought it was worth the extra couple of hours to drive into Florida. Gulf Shores was pretty special by any measure, but it wasn't as sophisticated as Destin.

Sure, each side of the highway was dotted with the traditional beach shops, replete with thousands of T-shirts, beach chairs, and umbrellas, but for every Alvin's Island, Destin boasted an upscale boutique for furniture, clothing, and art.

Sam couldn't resist heading to the Silver Sands outlet mall. Maybe it was a man thing; having more than one hundred stores all in one place was too convenient. Besides, whether it was true or not, Sam thought he was saving money by shopping at outlet stores.

Maggie said, "Would you mind if we made a quick stop at the Local Market and split a sandwich?"

Sam said, "If you like turkey and you like avocado, then we are in business."

The service was quick and friendly, and Maggie couldn't help wondering if they knew Sam from his professional life or just as a regular in Destin. After a quick sandwich, some yummy coleslaw, and a drink, they were on their way again.

Once again, Sam was right. This was a mega-outlet mall, with all the top brands, including Polo, Coach, Banana Republic, Ann Taylor, Saks—the list went on and on. To Maggie, it was the who's who of upscale shopping.

"We can shop until we drop," Sam said. "Or a couple of hours, whichever comes first."

Maggie couldn't help but laugh.

"But this is all about you, Maggie. Where do you want to go first? I'm going to stop in at the Polo store at some point, grab a few things, and I'll be ready to go. I'll be happy to go with you to whatever store you like."

A man who wants to go shopping? That's about as rare as a Tyrannosaurus in a zoo, Maggie thought. *When we date each other, we have a tendency to do all kinds of crazy things that we don't really mean. We do it just to impress each other. So does Sam want to go shopping—or does he like to go shopping? No matter, right now, at this time, at this place, he wants to go shopping and he even appears to like giving his opinion on different outfits.*

It had been too long since Maggie had been shopping. The last thing she had bought was a black dress to wear to David's funeral. That was not a happy memory. Maggie had never been obsessed with shopping for clothes. She liked looking nice, no doubt about it, but spending hours and hours in boutiques looking for that special pair of jeans or that "got-to-have-it" top was never her thing. She loved the idea of a good deal, but it seemed everything was always on sale in some form or fashion these days.

Today is going to be different, Maggie thought. *I am going with the flow. I am going to enjoy myself. I am going to let Sam spoil me a little.* "What should I wear to dinner this evening?"

"Believe it or not, a pair of shorts and a sleeveless top," Sam said.

"So the Oceanside restaurant isn't chichi?"

"Just the opposite. It's very down-to-earth, but I do want you to buy a couple of dresses while we are here, some shoes, maybe a new purse. Whatever you like."

Maggie liked that idea. She also liked the fact that Sam had good taste in clothes. As they ventured from store to store, Maggie discovered she and Sam had a similar philosophy when it came to fashion. She leaned more to the tried-and-true traditional, and so did Sam. *This is fun, but like all fun, it has to end sometime.*

After Sam made a brief stop at the Polo store—he knew exactly what he wanted and where it was in the store—they headed back to the beach house. Maggie couldn't wait to get back to the house and try on a few things for Sam.

After about twenty minutes, Maggie emerged like she had been a professional runway model for most of her life. She walked up and down in front of Sam so he could see her pale green sleeveless top paired with a classic pair of dark blue shorts. Her new, tan summer sandals were the perfect match. Like everything else, Maggie kept her jewelry simple but elegant. Her diamond earrings were understated, and a simple gold cross on a gold chain hung around her neck. "How do I look?"

"No matter what you are wearing, you look beautiful to me," Sam said. "I wouldn't even care if you didn't wear makeup. You always look beautiful to me."

"I don't know if I'll ever get an honest opinion from you, but, hey, I can live with having an admirer all day, every day."

"That is my honest, objective opinion. You are the most beautiful, wonderful, talented, capable, sincere, loving, caring person I know or will ever know."

"That sounds objective, all right. I'd hate to hear a biased statement if that is objective."

"That's the best I can do, Maggie."

"You aren't going to hear me complain."

"You about ready to go to dinner?"

In Brazil, Sam would often close his eyes and imagine walking at the edge of the water, hot sand under his feet and cool waves rushing toward him. In that moment, he would think about being with Maggie, walking together, holding hands, and talking of little things.

More than anything, Sam was glad he and Maggie were in Destin. It wasn't the Mediterranean, St. John, or even Laguna Beach in California, but it was a great beach—his favorite beach. After all, Sam had seen a lot of beaches in a lot of countries, but there was something special about the beach in Destin. It had a crazy combination of sophistication and simplicity. It was the perfect blend for Sam.

It was a place for families—husbands, wives, and children. Grandfathers and grandmothers. It wasn't the destination for the superrich. Just solid, down-to-earth people who loved the magnetism of the ocean.

Sure, some of the college crowd came to Destin in the spring, but it was minor league compared to other spring break destinations. And there were a lot of tourists and traffic in the summer months, but every beach has tourists and traffic. What city of any size didn't have traffic?

Maggie allowed herself to daydream. What if she and Sam hadn't gone their separate ways forty years ago? What if they had continued to date? What if they had married? How would her life be different today? But Maggie couldn't allow herself that luxury. She and David did have some good years. And she had Lucy and Lily. She was here, and now Maggie knew it was go time. She was almost sure Sam was going to propose marriage in a formal way at dinner. She had to have an answer. Sam deserved that much. Even if her answer was no, but what should she do?

There were so many ways to assess the situation. Sam was someone she had known for more than forty years. Or she could say, Sam was someone who she had really known only a few months. This was a man who came back into her life like a comet racing toward earth. Was this the most romantic moment of her life—or was this a con artist who was just too good to be true? Sam said she should trust him that everything was going to be fine. Maggie had a husband who told her the same thing—and look at how that ended.

Would Sam be a good stepdad to Lily and Lucy? Wow, stepdad? It was difficult for Maggie to contemplate the thought. Whatever the twins called Sam, would they really and truly accept him? Perhaps Sam was right—Lily and Lucy certainly wanted their mom to be happy.

All of a sudden, too many thoughts were racing through Maggie's mind. One thing at a time. She enjoyed the day and would try to enjoy the night. She didn't have to make a decision until Sam proposed for real. Then, Maggie had to admit, it would become very real. Was she ready to be Maggie Roberts? There would be a time, Maggie knew, when she couldn't delay her decision any longer. No decision would ultimately be a decision. It was inevitable. Maggie knew she had to summon the courage to make one of the biggest decisions of her life.

Chapter 13

"Oh my God, Sam, so this is our oceanside restaurant? You are right; it is breathtaking!"

In her wildest dreams, Maggie never would have guessed that was what Sam had in mind when he asked her to dinner. When he said oceanside, he meant oceanside. About a hundred feet from the edge of the water, a small dining table was anchored in the sand.

The heavy wooden table was covered with a pure white tablecloth. A pair of white candles in simple gold-leaf holders added a hint of elegance. Two wicker high-backed chairs were on each side of the table, along with a place setting for two. Maggie noticed the simplicity of the off-white bone china, along with traditional sterling silverware. She suspected the crystal water glass, as well as champagne flute, were Waterford. A bottle of champagne—not too expensive—probably Korbel, was icing next to the table.

It was the most romantic, intimate setting Maggie could ever imagine. She didn't care that every tourist within a mile could stare at them. *If that's how they want to spend their evening.*

The only time she was going to take her eyes off of Sam was to watch the sun set across the waves. The sound of the ocean was rhythmic and soothing; low humidity made the evening warm, but it was not overwhelmingly hot. Maggie was grateful to be in her pale green, sleeveless top and dark blue shorts.

"I know it's trite, but you shouldn't have done all this," Maggie said. She understood it was Sam's way of telling the world how much she meant to him.

"Do you really mean that?"

"I think it's the most wonderful thing anyone has ever done for me. I'll never forget this night."

"I've thought about this night for so many years." Sam rolled up the sleeves on his pink dress shirt. "I wanted this evening to be perfect. You sitting across from me. The sunset. The ocean. What we would eat. What we would drink. Every detail."

"I don't care what we eat or drink. This is perfect." While Maggie was gazing into Sam's eyes, she didn't notice a man in a tuxedo standing just behind her.

The waiter quickly moved to the side of the table,

halfway between Sam and Maggie. "Good evening, Mr. Roberts. I'm pleased to serve you this evening."

"Maggie, this is Raymond."

"Hello, Raymond." Maggie was a little bit overwhelmed and at a loss for words.

"It's a pleasure to meet you, Mrs. Duncan. You are just as lovely as Mr. Roberts said you were."

"Thanks to both of you. Please call me Maggie."

"If you need anything at all, Maggie, just let me know." Raymond opened the champagne, poured each of them a glass, and then disappeared as quickly as he had appeared.

"I would like to propose a toast," Sam said, raising his flute.

At that moment, Maggie and Sam were blinded by what appeared to be dozens of flashes of light. They were so busy concentrating on each other that they failed to notice the crowd that had gathered around their table. The lights were the flashes of cell phones capturing the moment. Instead of being irritated, all they could do was laugh.

"You are a celebrity—enjoy it," Sam said. "This is your fifteen minutes of fame."

They both hoisted their flutes and toasted the amateur paparazzi. Another round of flashes flowed over them, and then the crowd broke out in applause.

"Thank you, all. I guess you can tell I'm madly in love

with this woman. I'm glad you could share this with us. Have a good night." It wasn't the first crowd Sam had to wrangle, but he knew most people will be polite if you just treat them with respect. Sam knew they would go about their business soon enough, and he was right.

"See, I kept my promise. That was our first photo together—but hopefully not our last. Here is a toast to you, Maggie. May you find happiness the rest of your life."

As Sam and Maggie raised their glasses in a toast, a single tear trickled down Maggie's cheek. It was difficult for her to speak. "This is the most wonderful gift from a most wonderful man. Thank you for this evening and for being patient with me."

They each took a sip of champagne.

"Look." Sam's eyes turned toward the setting sun and the water.

Sam and Maggie could still feel the warmth of the sun, even though it was about to plunge into the ocean. The giant orange sphere was almost surreal as it hung just above the horizon.

"Destin has the most beautiful sunsets," Sam said. "Can we watch until it disappears?"

They sat in silence, hoping the sun would hang on the water's edge forever. If the sun never disappeared, maybe the night could last forever, too.

Sam took Maggie's hand in his and squeezed. Once the sun was gone, he turned and looked once again into her eyes. "It's just the two of us now—and the ocean, of course."

"What more could a girl want?" Maggie thought, *If only I was a girl again. I would have changed so many decisions.* It was difficult, but Maggie knew she had to think in the future tense and not the past tense.

As Sam's eyes adjusted, he caught Maggie's face in the candlelight. Her hair was pulled back in a twist, just like the first night he ever saw her. Still, he liked the woman he was with more than the young girl he fell in love with so many years ago.

Raymond reappeared with two shrimp cocktails, and Maggie suddenly discovered she was famished.

A crisp Caesar salad was next, followed by the piece de resistance: fresh swordfish baked in lemon butter, roasted potatoes, and sautéed asparagus. Dessert was a favorite of both Sam and Maggie: crème brûlée.

"I couldn't eat another bite," Maggie said. "It was the best dinner I've ever had, and that's not even counting the wonderful food. This is so special, Sam. Thank you."

"You made it special, Maggie. I would never have done it without you. I am hoping we can do it again for our twenty-fifth wedding anniversary."

"That's being very optimistic, don't you think?"

"Are you talking about marriage or our age?"

"I meant at our age."

"So you *will* marry me?"

"I didn't say that either."

Maggie could see the disappointed look in Sam's eyes.

"I've been saving this night to tell you how I really feel," Sam said. "As if you don't already know."

Maggie knew this must be the moment.

"I love you with all my heart, Maggie. All my soul. Since the day we met, you have been with me. I've always loved you—and only you. And I always will love only you. When I close my eyes, I can smell your hair. I can see your special smile. I can taste your lips on mine. And now I know what it's like to sleep beside you and hold you in my arms."

Maggie had loved their Friday night together, lying next to each other and holding on for dear life.

"I want to marry you, Maggie. I want us to be together for the rest of our lives. I don't want another day to go by without you. I've wasted too many days without you already."

"In your world, when would this happen, Sam?"

"How about tomorrow, the next day, or the day after that? You tell me."

"We don't even have a license; how could we get married."

Always the practical one, Maggie thought to herself.

"We have the Lear, and more importantly, I have connections in Brazil. I know a priest there who would marry us. We could be back a day later."

"Lucy and Lily. I would want them there."

"I can send for them—if you like—or we could have another ceremony when we return."

"You certainly have all the answers, don't you?"

"I've only had forty years to plan this. There is one other thing we need to discuss." Sam hesitated for a moment.

"Really? Don't scare me, Sam."

"No more surprises, no secrets. Full disclosure," Sam said.

"You mean like the scholarships you gave the twins?" Maggie couldn't help herself.

"They earned every penny of those scholarships—and you know it!"

"Okay. No more argument about the scholarships. That's been settled."

"Good."

"So?"

"I don't need to tell you this, and, in truth, I wish I didn't have to discuss this, but we need to because you have brought it up a couple of times. This isn't a big deal to me, but I'm going to tell you anyway."

"You can just stop speaking in code and just tell me, for

goodness' sake." This time, it was Maggie's turn to use a half-serious, half-joking tone.

"You've asked a couple of times about money. If you would have to support me—or us."

"You don't have to—"

"I have some money. A lot of money, actually. All the stars aligned for me, and it just worked out that way."

"Did you win the Brazilian version of the lottery?"

"Nothing like that. The stock market. When you don't have a family and you make a ridiculous salary, you can invest a good chunk of it. I played the market in the 1990s. I decided to risk it all. I gambled, and I won. As you may or may not know, the stock market went crazy during the 1990s."

"So you could lose it all at any time?"

"Not exactly. I changed strategies at the end of the century. I went conservative at just the right time, thanks to my investment counselor."

"It's your money, Sam. If money mattered to me, I would have done something other than teach part-time at a university."

"I know. I just wanted you to know you don't have to worry about supporting me. In fact, there's enough for our lifetime, the life span of Lucy and Lily, and well as your grandchildren, when they come along. I just want you to understand in case it comes up again."

"Why would it come up again?"

"I have attorneys, and they will insist you sign a prenuptial agreement before we get married."

"There can't be that much money."

"I think I should tell you—even though it's tacky."

"Your money is your business, Sam. I don't need to know. Can we drop it now?"

"No. Because there's not going to be a prenuptial agreement. All my money will go to you and your girls, except what we give to charity, of course. It's over a hundred million dollars."

Surely Maggie didn't hear Sam correctly. It must have been the waves crashing against the shore.

"The last thing I need is another complication," Maggie said. "If we get married, I would be happy if we had money for the basics—food, clothes, a house, a car."

"We have money for the basics," Sam said.

"Maybe we won't if you keep spending money like you did this weekend."

"I also promise we aren't going to fly in private jets our entire life. This weekend is a once-in-a-lifetime kind of thing."

"I must confess, I'm enjoying every minute of this, Sam. I'm glad you did this. It's beyond my wildest dreams."

"I'm glad we could have this night together, but it's not over yet."

"There's more?"

"A little more. I'll be back in a minute or two." Sam sprung to his feet and disappeared into the dark of night. Within a few minutes, he was back with a half dozen people carrying musical instruments.

"May I have this dance?" Sam asked, pulling Maggie to her feet.

The group's first song was an instrumental. The melody was familiar to Maggie, but she couldn't quite place it. It was the first time she had heard it played with violins and cello.

"You may want to take off your shoes when you step onto the dance floor," Sam suggested, slipping off his tan boat shoes.

"I did that hours ago."

Sam took Maggie into his arms, moving slowly to the music, and he held her tightly around the waist with his right hand, his other hand coupled in hers. The candles on the table gave off just enough light so they could look deeply into each other's eyes.

Maggie gently placed her head on Sam's shoulder. He

could feel the softness of her hair and smell the sweetness of her skin. The sand was cool to their feet, but their embrace warmed every fiber of their bodies.

Then it hit her.

"That's the last song we ever danced to all those years ago, isn't it?"

Sam nodded.

"All those years ago—and you remembered?" *I can't believe it.*

Sam wanted to say something, but the lump in his throat wouldn't let him. Instead, he just held her, moving from side to side to the music and the waves.

The band kept playing "St. James Infirmary" a second time, but Sam and Maggie didn't mind.

As long as the band played, they danced, holding each other close. When the song was over, they clapped in appreciation.

"How about playing Maggie's favorite song?" Sam asked the leader of the group.

"You remember my favorite song?"

"It's been so long, and you might have another favorite song by now."

"I don't. It's the same one."

"Then, if you would do me the honor of one more dance."

Sam took Maggie's hand in his, striking another classic dance position, and then he nodded to the band.

The group began to play "Somewhere Over the Rainbow," and the lead female vocalist sang each note with great emotion.

Not a word was said during the entire song. Sam nuzzled his check against Maggie's forehead. They both closed their eyes and lost themselves in the moment.

After the final note was sung, Maggie stood on her toes and kissed Sam on the lips. The kiss lingered for a minute. This time, it was the band's turn to applaud.

"Since we did my favorite song, can we do your favorite song?" *One good turn deserves another.* "I'm sorry, but I can't remember your favorite song. Can we see if our group of musicians know it?"

"Do you know 'Moon River'?" Sam asked.

"No problem, Mr. Roberts," the vocalist said.

As the band began to play, Maggie put both hands around Sam's neck and stared at him. *He has to be the most generous, kind person I've ever met.* "I do love you, Sam."

"I love you, Maggie. More than you could ever imagine."

Maggie and Sam couldn't tell when the song had ended and the next one began. They didn't want to let go of each other; they didn't want the night to end. It was the perfect evening.

Sam finally said, "Could we sit for a minute?"

"If you like."

As soon as Maggie was seated, Sam knelt on one knee, reached into his pocket, took out a tiny box, and handed it to Maggie.

"Sam ..." Maggie took the box from his hand and opened it. The diamond ring was a classic round stone in a gold setting. It was just like Maggie—down-to-earth but elegant.

"I want you to have this even if you decide to return to Louisiana without me. I want you to remember me and remember this weekend."

"It's so beautiful, Sam."

"I want us to be husband and wife forever. I never want to leave you—not for a day but for the rest of my life."

"I do love you, Sam. More than you will know. Please believe me. I love you, but I don't deserve you."

"Never, ever say that again. I can't imagine us having a fight, but I might start one if you say anything like that again. You deserve so much. You are a wonderful person. Caring. Bright. Beautiful. A terrific mother."

"Thank you for your vote of confidence. You are a wonderful man. Handsome. Smart. You think of others before you think of yourself."

"See, we have so much in common." Sam chuckled. "It would be a sin if we didn't get married."

"I certainly can't afford another sin right now," Maggie said, her voice dripping with her dry wit.

"You know how much I love you. I can't bear to think of living without you ever again. You are in me, and I believe I am in you."

"At this moment, I couldn't be happier, Sam. More than anything, know how happy I am. I promise I'll give you an answer first thing tomorrow morning. Just give me one more night to sleep on it. Don't forget that you've loved me for forty years—and I've loved you for all of seventy-two hours."

"Fair enough. Would you like to take a short walk down the beach before we go back to the house?"

"Only if you promise we don't have to have any more weighty discussions."

Sam rolled up his off-white linen pants, put his shoes in his right hand, and took Maggie's hand in his.

Maggie left her shoes under the table. "Where would we live if we were married?"

"I thought you didn't want to have another heavy-duty discussion tonight?" Sam couldn't help himself. "Anywhere you want. We can live in Natchitoches, or here at the beach, or any beach, for that matter. New York, London, San

Francisco, Venice. Any continent. Any country. Any state. Anywhere. You may want to see where the twins settle before we make that decision."

"I guess that narrows it down for me. Maybe I asked the wrong question. If you could live anywhere, where would you live?"

"Right here in Destin. I've seen a lot of cities in my career, but there's something special about this place. And, as you know, I love the beach most of all."

"And we would live in your house?"

"We could sell this one and have one of our own. We could live on the beach, off the beach, you decide."

"I've always wanted to live on the beach."

"On the beach, it is then. As long as you are with me, I will be happy. So what would we do if we did live at the beach?"

"I like giving back, so I was hoping we could do volunteer work—really trying to do a little bit to give back to the community. What would you like to do?"

"That sounds great," Sam said. "As a learned philosopher once told me, 'As long as we are together.'"

"I'm not quite ready to leave Natchitoches just yet. I have a few more years before I retire. Besides, I love my work at the university."

"I thought you might want to stay. Having deep roots in

a community is a good thing. In the meantime, we could come to the beach whenever your schedule allowed."

"Even though I have some horrible memories in Natchitoches, I also have some good ones."

"I'm ready to settle down in one place—if that is with you in Natchitoches or here in Destin. I've lived too many places, too many big cities. I like the idea of a smaller place to call home."

"Like you said, we need to see where Lily and Lucy end up living. They may be in the same city, probably not. Besides, I would be hesitant to move close to them at first. They could move—and then what would we do?"

"I think we are getting a little ahead of ourselves. Better to take this one step at a time." Sam looked up and saw the most beautiful crescent moon. "But we could visit them as much as you like."

"If we live here in Destin, we might not have to visit them all that much. My guess is that they would want to visit us all the time. They love the beach as much as we do—so they would be begging for an invitation to hang out at the beach."

"Even better."

"I know they will love you, Sam."

"I can't wait to get to know them. I hope I can spend

even more time with them as soon as we get back from our honeymoon."

"Honeymoon? That never even crossed my mind."

"I love to travel. Our honeymoon would be our first official big trip together. We could go to Europe, Asia, Africa, the East Coast, the West Coast, or somewhere in between. The world is our oyster."

"We would have to postpone our honeymoon for a while. My semester starts pretty soon."

"If we go to Asia, maybe we could go see the twins either coming or going."

"They would love that, I know."

"Don't forget, we want them to be at the wedding. When we get married, maybe we could take a day and just look around where I lived in Brazil. I would like for you to meet my friends and see a bit of the country. I would love for you to see the work we were doing there."

"Are you sure you don't want to or need to return to live in Brazil?"

"I'm sure. I promise. It was time for me to come back to America. If we are married in Brazil, it would give me a chance to say goodbye."

"I'm sure all your friends there would like to say goodbye to you. You need that, and so do they."

"You are so wise."

"Wise. That's a word you use to describe old people. I thought we were just getting started."

"I hope we are. I really hope we are." Sam let Maggie's words sink in for a minute.

Sam turned to face Maggie and took her face in his hands. "I love you so much it hurts." He gave her a tender kiss on the forehead, then her left cheek, then the right cheek, and finally, he pressed his lips to hers.

They walked back to the beach house with their arms around each other's waists.

"Are you sleepy?" Maggie asked.

"Not very sleepy, but, yes, I'm dog tired."

Before Sam could say another word, Maggie put her hand over his mouth and gently kissed is face. "Can we cuddle and sleep together tonight?" Maggie had mixed emotions about her question, but she wanted to suggest it as a possibility. She wanted to sleep with Sam, but she also knew she had promised to give him a decision first thing in the morning. *A promise is a promise, and I am going to keep this one for sure.*

"Since you need time to think, why don't you take one of the upstairs bedrooms," Sam said.

"Are you kicking me out of bed already?" Maggie asked with a wry smile.

"No way. I thought it would give you some time to yourself, to think. Without me."

"I'm just kidding. As my grandmother used to say, 'If I didn't love you, I wouldn't kid you.' I think separate bedrooms are a good idea. It's going to give me a few hours to finally decide what I want to do and why."

Maggie couldn't help but see a little disappointment on Sam's face. "Remember, this was your suggestion, Sam."

"I'm not disappointed about sleeping in separate rooms. I just wish you had already made your decision to marry me."

"I know. I know. It's going to be fine. You have given me a lot to think about in the past few days. I'm asking you to trust me. I'll make the best decision I can for myself, my girls, and for you. I promise. And, don't worry, I totally understand this is a two-way street. You could wake up tomorrow and decide getting married isn't what you want to do at all. I may not be the one for you. I may be too high-maintenance. This may be too much, especially since you've never been married before. You may wake up tomorrow and tell me God is calling you back to Brazil. Who knows what tomorrow will bring?"

"You aren't high-maintenance, but even if you were, I'm committed to you."

"That's why I care for you so much, Sam. You want me no matter what. Warts and all. No conditions. There's probably not a woman in the world who doesn't think I'm crazy right now. Most women would get on that jet right now and never look back. Most women would never think twice about a man who is good—not to mention handsome and rich."

"The sooner we go to bed, the sooner it will be morning," Sam said.

No matter what happens, Sam thought, *finding Maggie was worth the risk. I will never forget this weekend. If Maggie goes back to her old life, I will be heartbroken, no doubt about it, but I will try to understand.* What he had learned at Catholic school so long ago would serve him well in his adult life. *God never gives you more than you can handle. If Maggie decides we shouldn't be together, it will put that belief to the test.*

Sam didn't know exactly how he would react if Maggie decided to return to Natchitoches and leave him behind, but he knew he couldn't bear to get back on the jet without her. He would send her back alone, and he would remain at the beach house.

Beyond Maggie, Sam hadn't thought about the next step in his life. Maybe he would go back to Brazil and work a little longer until he could figure out what to do. He would keep the house in Destin because there would be a day when he would return and live out his life near the ocean.

Still, something would be missing. Sam couldn't think

of life without Maggie. Failing had never been in his vocabulary, but this decision was out of his hands. From the moment he arrived at Maggie's front door, he knew there was a possibility that she could reject him. Of course, it would have been easier if that had happened right away.

It would be difficult, but Sam wasn't going to dwell on the negative. He didn't want to give life to an idea that would be devastating. No, he would think positively. Optimistically. He would approach this situation like he did most situations in his life. He would continue to believe good things happen to good people. At least, he hoped good things happened to him and Maggie.

In the end, Sam decided, *everything will work out for the best.*

"I'll say good night," Sam said as he hugged Maggie. "Take any of the upstairs rooms."

"Good night, Sam. Sweet dreams. Thanks again for a great day—and night."

"No doubt we need a good night's rest." For the first time since he arrived, he lied to Maggie. There was no way he was going to get a good night's sleep. The morning couldn't come soon enough.

Chapter 14

Maybe it was a bad dream—a very bad dream. The night seemed like a thousand hours. Sam would sleep for an hour or two, wake up for an hour or two, and then doze off again. Now he was awake. He was sure of it, but what he faced was more than a bad dream—it was a nightmare.

When he first opened his eyes, it was difficult for Sam to focus. He was on his side, facing the nightstand. He thought he saw his name in bold script. Maybe he was wrong. Maybe it was a dream. So he shook his head, clearing the morning fog from his eyes. He wasn't wrong. There was a note propped up on the nightstand, and it had his name on it. With his hand shaking like a 7.3 earthquake, Sam ripped open the envelope.

Sam —

I'm sorry. I had to leave.

Maggie

No, this isn't a nightmare. This is a disaster of epic proportions. What a fool! After the most wonderful night of my life, this happens? Six words: "I'm sorry. I had to leave." No explanation, no nothing. Just goodbye.

Sam leaped to his feet, threw on his shorts, and raced out of his bedroom. He raced around the beach house and searched for Maggie. The Wagoneer was still outside. *Maybe Maggie didn't really leave. Is this some cruel joke—or did Maggie decide she couldn't face me? Is this her way out? And she called me a coward? I feel like a parent whose daughter runs away from home. One minute, you panic, wondering— hoping—she is alive and well. The next minute, you are mad, ready to scold her. The minute after that, you just want to find her and give her a hug because she is safe.*

Calm down. Don't panic. Sam took a few deep breaths, sat down on the front steps of the beach house, and tried to think. *How could she do this—and without a single word? I never had a chance to plead my case one last time. Perhaps that is exactly why she left the note without saying anything. Maggie didn't want to talk. She just wanted to leave.*

Down at the ocean, Sam saw Jack casting his line. *Maybe Jack knows something.* Sam vaulted off the front steps and headed for the beach. "Jack, Jack, have you seen Maggie this morning?"

"Yes, sir, as a matter of fact, I have. I drove her to the airport. She said she was catching a plane back home."

"Did she say anything else?" Like a good detective, Sam wanted to gather every bit of information possible.

"No, sir. Not much. Just the usual polite conversation people have. You know, 'It looks like another day in paradise.' Stuff like that."

"How long ago did you drop her off?"

"It's been a couple of hours."

Sam thought about going to the airport to find Maggie, but he knew it wouldn't be any use. *Two hours is a long time. By the time I get there, she would be long gone back to Louisiana. It can't hurt to check flight times.* He was right. By nine o'clock, every flight to Shreveport was already in the air. The only thing worse Sam could possibly hear was that a plane had crashed—and Maggie was on it. Now there was nothing to do but wait. Wait and worry. Worry and wait.

Sam felt like his life had crashed and burned. Even worse, he didn't understand what was going through Maggie's mind. This was the same woman who seemed so positive just a few hours earlier. Every vibe from Maggie told Sam that she was ready for them to be together for the rest of their lives. This was the same woman he had held in his arms and smothered with kisses. This was the same woman who had taken him to another dimension. This was the same woman who had told Sam she loved him—and more than once. Sam had believed her. He had believed every word.

Sam's instinct was to get back on the Lear. *I could follow Maggie back to her house, but this might not be the best time to follow my instincts. Maggie obviously needs some time to think—or perhaps she doesn't. Perhaps she made up her mind and decided to go back to her old life—a life without me.*

The only thing Sam could do was give her space. The waiting would be torture. Sam didn't know if he could stand it, but what choice did he have? What was the next move? Stay in Destin for a few days or go back to Brazil. Really get away and hope that, at some point, Maggie would reach out to him. Maggie had his cell number. If she wanted to call, she would. It might take a few days. It might take six months. Sam had to be prepared for Maggie to never speak to him again.

Brazil seemed to be the best option. Go back, get his things, and then come back to the beach and see what happens. *One day at a time,* Sam thought. He had often heard other people talk about what it means to take one day at a time, but this was the first time he had experienced that feeling himself. One day at a time was hard, but it was the only option.

Sam was smart enough to know Maggie leaving forever was a possibility. You can try to be a grown-up, but when you get punched in the gut, it still hurts. Sam already missed Maggie terribly. It was all Sam could do to hold back his emotions. It was no use. He sat down on the couch, put his face in his hands, and began to sob.

For the first time in his lifetime, Sam was frozen in place. He couldn't think, he couldn't breathe, and he couldn't function. He was a far cry from the steely veteran broadcaster with millions of fans across the country—and around the world. No amount of celebrity could help him now. He had never felt more alone. For three hours, Sam didn't move. He didn't think, he didn't eat, and he barely blinked. He knew he had to get a grip. He had to snap out of it and make a decision—even if it was a bad decision.

The best thing to do, Sam thought, *is to get out of Dodge— and fast.* Before he knew it, he was dialing the number of his pilot. It wasn't rational, but Sam didn't care at this point.

"Let's get this jet cranked up and head for Brazil," Sam said. "I want to be in Brazil as soon as possible."

"Give me one hour, and I'll be ready to go," the pilot said.

Sam put his phone on the glass coffee table and stared

out the window toward nothing in particular. Losing the woman you love once in your life is bad enough, but losing the woman you love twice in your lifetime is more than a man could bear. Putting some distance between himself and Maggie might help. Sam knew it wouldn't, but he didn't see any other choice.

Sam didn't have much to pack. He threw the few things he had in an overnight bag, and within minutes, Sam and Jack were headed to the airport. The engines of the Lear cranked up, and the pilot put the aircraft through all of his preflight routine.

To Sam's surprise, the pilot shut down both engines. "I'm so sorry, Mr. Roberts, but we have a problem with the hydraulic system. We are getting a negative reading on our instrument check."

"And?"

"And it looks like we'll have to be here for a while until we can get a mechanic to look it over. Safety first, sir, especially if we are going all the way to South America."

"How long will it take?"

"I'd say no more than five or six hours at the most."

"Five or six hours? I don't have five or six hours." It was unusual for Sam to raise his voice in anger to anyone. "I'm sorry. I shouldn't take it out on you just because I'm in a horrible mood."

"Apology accepted, Mr. Roberts. I think I understand what you are going through. If it's an assurance, I think everything is going to be all right."

You have no earthly idea what I'm going through—and you have no idea if everything is going to be all right. Sam decided to keep his thoughts to himself.

"Why don't you go back to the beach house and relax," the pilot said. "I'll call you as soon as this ship is ready to fly."

Sam had always thought of his beach house as a sanctuary. He remembered the day he signed the papers. It was sunny and a cool seventy-two degrees. Slight wind blowing. Blue-green water glistening, calling him like the song of the sirens. He sat on the front porch that afternoon without a care in the world. Life was better than good. His career was going gangbusters, and he was in a good place in his personal life. He didn't have the one person he wanted, but there was nothing he could do about Maggie at that moment. He just wanted to sit and be mesmerized by the smell of the salty air.

There was a lot of decorating left to do, but that was minor compared to owning the house. He wanted to make it a home, and he didn't mind spending the money to make it feel cozy and inviting. Sam didn't even mind spending time alone at the beach. After all, he had gotten used to the idea of spending the rest of his life as a bachelor. He was one of the most eligible bachelors in the United States, but that wouldn't last. Every year there would be someone more handsome, richer, and more charismatic. He never took it seriously.

Sam realized he had just been fooling himself all this time. Yes, the house was great—impeccable, in fact. Yes, Destin was gorgeous—his favorite beach with sugary-white sand and crystal clear water, but once Maggie set foot inside, he knew it was different. Before it was just a hollow shell of a dream. His house needed one more ingredient: the love he could give Maggie and the love Maggie could give him. Such a beautiful home needed laughter, scented candles, and homemade chocolate chip cookies.

Walking up the front steps, Sam knew the beach house was the last place he wanted to be at the moment. *What am I going to do?* He didn't feel like taking a nap, even though he was dead tired. Eating was the last thing on his mind. He didn't even want to sit out on the deck. Even the ocean had lost all of her charm. The only thing left was to try to figure out why Maggie had left. Why did she leave that cryptic note and vanish?

Maybe I'm being selfish, Sam thought. *Maybe Maggie had a good excuse for leaving so suddenly. Maybe there was some sort of emergency with the twins or a friend in Natchitoches.*

Maybe there just wasn't a second to waste and not a moment to leave a detailed explanation. If that were the case, why wouldn't Maggie just wake me up and say goodbye? What would a minute or two either way mean in the scheme of things?

Sam couldn't think of any other reason that made sense. *Maggie probably didn't want to take the risk of speaking to me face-to-face. She probably couldn't bear to see the look of disappointment on my face. She is probably hurting, too.*

Sam decided to take his mind to another dimension. He sat in a leather easy chair and tried to think of nothing at all. He figured it was his only defense. After a while, Sam drifted off. He was so tired. It wasn't a deep sleep, but it allowed him to survive for now. When he awoke, he felt even worse. He was depressed and groggy.

He promised himself he wouldn't go after Maggie—or even try to call her. The next move had to come from Maggie. Sam decided on a compromise plan. He would write her a letter. Writing would be cathartic. After all, it's what he did best all those years in the business. He kept writing paper and a pen in his desk drawer.

> My Dearest Maggie —
> I can't tell you how much I miss you. I don't understand why you left this morning. Couldn't you have stayed just long enough to give me some sort of explanation?

I know I told you to do what you think is best for you and the twins, but I thought the weekend went wonderfully. I guess I was wrong. I must say, I didn't see this coming. I'm a big boy, but it still hurts.

If you need more time, I understand. Well, maybe I don't really understand, but I want to try to understand. Just talk to me. Tell me what you are thinking.

I truly believe you love me—and you know I love you. We can work through this. I know it. Just as important, we are friends. Friends are there for each other, and I want to be there for you.

Even though we are apart, I'm with you in spirit. I always have been. That hasn't changed. I will always be with you. I love you a thousand times a thousand.

Yours forever,

Sam

The last thing Sam wanted to do was put his letter in the mail. Maybe the best thing for him to do was just tear it up and not give it to Maggie at all. Sam felt better after writing it, but perhaps the right thing to do was put it in the wastebasket.

If he was going to send it, he needed to make sure it didn't get lost somehow. It would be better delivered in person. And if he was going to deliver it in person, he might as well try to talk with Maggie in person rather than just dropping it through the mail slot on her front door.

Forget the letter, Sam thought. *Go to Natchitoches and confront Maggie. It is the only way I will know for sure what is happening. After all, just two days ago, Maggie told me I should stand up for my convictions.*

His head was pounding from too many thoughts swirling around in his brain. Sam heard a faint sound. After a few seconds, he recognized the ring tone of his cell phone. *Maybe it is Maggie.*

"Mr. Roberts, the plane is ready to fly," the pilot said. "It only took four and a half hours instead of five."

Sam was in no mood for any kind of joke from his pilot. "I'll be there as soon as I can. File your flight plan for Natchitoches instead of Brazil."

"Yes, sir."

It was time for Sam to fight for the woman he loved.

When Sam arrived at the Lear, his heart was pounding even more than his head. He couldn't get to Natchitoches fast enough. He raced up the steps of the Lear, ducked his head, and stepped inside.

He froze—just like he had last Friday in front of Maggie's house. He couldn't move an inch.

"You still want to get married, Mr. Roberts?" Maggie was sitting in the passenger seat, smiling that big wonderful smile.

Sam, couldn't speak a word, but he could feel the tears welling up in his eyes.

"Will you be my husband forever and ever, Sam?"

"I will," Sam whispered, rushing to her arms. Sam was on his knees, and Maggie was leaning forward, holding him tightly.

Sam didn't want to let go. He was afraid if he ever let her go again, he might not ever see her.

Maggie could feel what he was thinking, and she felt a little ashamed.

"I swear I'll never leave you again," Maggie said. "Never. I promise."

Sam pulled away for a moment. "I was worried sick. Where …"

"A woman can't get married in Brazil without a passport, can she? Besides, I needed to pick up some extra clothes."

"You scared me to death, young lady."

"And for that, I am truly sorry. Will you forgive me this once? I was thinking your first reaction might be to return to Brazil, so I asked the pilot to pretend something was wrong with the plane until he could come back and retrieve me."

Sam glanced back at his pilot. "So you were in on this the whole time? And you let me twist in the wind? I should fire you on the spot, but then, we wouldn't have a pilot." Sam couldn't help but break into a slight grin.

"So I guess we won't be going to Natchitoches after all, Mr. Roberts," the pilot said.

"We don't need to go to Natchitoches—unless the future Mrs. Roberts needs more clothes. Head for Rio de Janeiro," Sam said.

"And the first priest you can find," Maggie added.

"I think we should renew our vows every year for the next hundred years," Sam said.

"And what about the twins?" Maggie asked.

"We can send for them immediately—if that's what you want."

"I would like that, and I think they would want to be there."

"There's only one problem having them with us when we get married," Sam said.

"And that would be?"

"After the ceremony, Lily and Lucy might not see us for three or four days—if you get my drift."

"I like your drift, Mr. Roberts."

Maggie and Sam sat next to each other, holding hands in silence, content in the moment. The Lear's engines began to roar as the jet moved down the runway.

"All that you claim to have, Sam—"

"What about it?"

"We are going to have a great time giving it away, aren't we?"

"We can sure try."

"I want you to know you are the only thing in the world that matters to me, Sam. I couldn't be happier, and I'm looking forward to a long and happy life with you."

Sam held Maggie's hand even tighter, and then he leaned over and gave her a warm, tender kiss. Sam could feel his heart in his throat—or maybe it was just the Lear slicing through the thick summer clouds, beginning its climb toward heaven.

Acknowledgments

When Kara Lee Ford and I attended the University of North Texas, we had stars in our eyes and hope for our future in journalism. Thankfully, both of us were able to fulfill our professional dreams. During our time at the university, we were in the same creative writing class. Of course, Kara Lee earned an A, while I managed a B. Now, our lives have come full circle, and here we are collaborating on *The Weekend*. Honestly, I couldn't have completed this project without her expertise and encouragement.

Kara Lee has been involved in journalism since she was editor of her high school newspaper in Phillips, Texas. While attending Frank Phillips Junior College, she worked as a reporter for the *Borger News-Herald*. As a college sophomore, she transferred to the University of North Texas and worked on the student newspaper for three years, serving as editor of the *North Texas Daily* her senior year. In 1972, she was the second female in the United States—and the first in Texas—to be elected president of a Sigma Delta Chi journalism fraternity and was named the University of North Texas Outstanding Senior Journalism Student.

Kara Lee continued her journalism career as a copy editor for the *Dallas Morning News* before moving into public relations with AT&T in Dallas in 1973. During her twenty-seven years with AT&T, she was transferred to St. Louis, back to Dallas, and then to Little Rock, Arkansas. In the past twenty years, Kara Lee has worked for two advertising agencies, the Arkansas Press Association, and the Arkansas Scholarship Lottery.

Coming Soon from Mike Whitehead

One in a Million

Elizabeth Goin was a numbers person, and her numbers added up to a life well lived. Number one in school, and number one at work. She was nearly perfect on her CPA exam. Part 1, check.

Five years is all it took for her to rise to senior vice president of a prestigious accounting firm in Dallas. Yes, life was indeed good. No, life was great. Now, at the age of thirty-three, Elizabeth was wondering what life would bring next. Was there room for a family now that all her boxes were checked?

Then came a number that Elizabeth didn't see coming—333 million. The improbable happened. Elizabeth Goin won the lottery—$333 million. Elizabeth knew the odds were astronomical, especially since this was the first time she had ever bought a lottery ticket, but something odd came over Elizabeth. Instead of being elated, she was deflated. For the first time in her life, she didn't know what to do. Because of her newfound wealth, she thought everyone would look at her in a different way—bad different, not good different.

And on top of that, her company hired a new consultant—Maximilian Moonlight. And it looked like the new consultant had been given one assignment: to fire the senior vice president. All of a sudden, her life was out of control. Elizabeth had to take a breath and buy some time. So she decided to put the lottery ticket in her safe-deposit box and wait. Elizabeth always had a plan, but now she needed a new one. She had a few months to decide what to do about her future, but first things first. She had to find a way to deal with one Mr. Maximilian Moonlight.

CPSIA information can be obtained
at www.ICGtesting.com
Printed in the USA
LVHW040928121121
702955LV00006B/194

9 781480 899803